THE BLACK CANDLE

With Chatton Eastwood's history of Satan worship, the locals believed that black magic was again rife. And witchcraft became a cover for premeditated murder. Children, playing in a quarry, found the body later identified as Amos White, missing since the theft of two priceless tapestries. But the real Amos was secretly buried in Drearden's Wood. His killer knew it — so did the blackmailer — as well as some inconvenient facts about a lot of people . . . And death could not fail to come again.

Books by Evelyn Harris
in the Linford Mystery Library:

DEADLY GREEN
LARGELY LUCK

EVELYN HARRIS

THE BLACK CANDLE

Complete and Unabridged

LINFORD
Leicester

First published in Great Britain
By Robert Hale Limited
London

First Linford Edition
published 2007
by arrangement with
Robert Hale Limited
London

British Library CIP Data

Harris, Evelyn
 The black candle.—Large print ed.—
 Linford mystery library
 1. Detective and mystery stories
 2. Large type books
 I. Title
 823.9′14 [F]

 ISBN 978–1–84617–714–9

Published by
F. A. Thorpe (Publishing)
Anstey, Leicestershire

Set by Words & Graphics Ltd.
Anstey, Leicestershire
Printed and bound in Great Britain by
T. J. International Ltd., Padstow, Cornwall

This book is printed on acid-free paper

1

His first impulse was to throw the knife away but, wiped of the blood, it was a good knife and, besides, it might be missed. Squatting on his heels in the shimmering moonlight, he thrust the blade again and again, up to its hilt, into the soft earth. The only patch of soft earth within miles around, he thought grimly, as he pocketed the weapon; and by morning that soil, too, would be frozen solid and undetectable from its surroundings. To make doubly sure, he tugged across some of the smaller debris scattered about; ice-enamelled branches and last autumn's leaves, and a thick, tangled mat of dead and bramble-woven vegetation. Not that anyone would be likely to come that way, not in these dark, coffin-like days of January, and by spring the disturbed ground would have disappeared as if it had never been; lost beneath the burgeoning undergrowth.

Open-mouthed, gasping, almost at the end of his strength, he gave a last heave to a broken bough and winced as the icy air sliced into his aching lungs. His breath hung like a shroud before his face, opaque in the moonlight. He felt hollowed by the cold. But this was a job he would do but once and he aimed to do it well, and neither outside discomfort nor the steady slam which had started up behind his eyes was going to stop him. Nor was there really any need for speed or concern: he had this post-midnight world to himself. Below freezing-point, and with a bitter wind, it was not the kind of night to encourage idle wanderers in the wood.

For a moment his frozen lips stirred into something approaching a smile. Drearden's Wood — even the name struck bleak — a sickle-shaped piece of rough woodland which bounded the village to the north-east. Apart from a couple of summer-trodden short cuts to the river, it was untracked; his undisputed territory in the dog days almost as much as now. This was his world, his country-side, his habitat, and he knew every oak and ash and birch, every polished holly and ancient yew; every rock and rut and deadfall. And he would travel quickly, heading home. Stepping back, he surveyed his handiwork with satisfaction. Nothing there to arouse suspicion; the woodland floor appeared as normal. And he bent to gather up the bundle near his feet.

Above his head the branches of the bare trees rattled together like dry old bones, letting through the moonlight in stuttering silver patches. Here, he was protected from the worst of the wind, but when he left the shelter of the trees he would, he knew, feel its true venom. Even now its moan in the boughs above him was increasing steadily, and chill gnawed him to the core. His exertions had drawn sweat but failed to heat him, and his teeth were chattering violently despite all efforts to control them. Yet whether that was from the cold or from some bodily reaction to the events of the past few hours, it was hard to say. What he craved for now was warmth, and a drink, and, above all, sleep. Sleep! A warm bed and a stiff drink and he would sleep like the dead. Again, that smile which was little more than a vague movement of the stiff blue lips.

Presently he turned and, leaving the hidden grave, began to pick his path back the way he had come, treading carefully from tree to tree, while brambles and low branches caught at him like claws.

He paused on the edge of the woodland to hitch his sacking-wrapped tools — the small pickaxe and the vicious cutting-spade — more comfortably upon his shoulder. The clink of metal against metal reminded him that it would not do for those tools to be missed. They must be returned to their shed before morning. Now. Before daylight brought activity.

Aware of the knife swinging heavily against his leg, he trotted forward into the full metallic glare of the moonlight. Beneath his boots the frozen grass of the field crunched crisp and uneven, its rough tussocks glittering here and there with the diamond-sparkle of ice, as, with swift strides, he made his way towards the gap in the hedge and the stile that gave access to the lane. But he never climbed it. When he grasped the top crossbar to vault over he saw his hands plainly for the first time in an uncompromising wash of light. They were covered in blood. At least, he guessed it to be blood. It had all the sticky wetness of blood, although it showed tarblack in the moonlight. He stared down, motionless. His blood? Or blood from the old man? It was difficult to tell if he were bleeding now, and he felt no pain. But conceivably he could have cut himself: the knife was sharp and the night, cold. Cold enough to deaden flesh.

On further examination he discovered that blood also smeared his arms and made an ugly stain across his chest. Dangerous to be seen like that. And stupid. But what to do? He wiped a trembling hand across his eyes. Fatigue had made his brain like butter. He was tired and he was cold, and his head ached fit to burst. Above all, he wanted to go home. Yet he would have to get cleaned up first, otherwise — The breath rasped in his throat as he felt the fierce tide of confidence ebbing away, panic rising.

What if someone should spot him? Unlikely, at this hour, but still . . .

He lifted his hand to his face again and held it there, paralysed. His face! How many times that night had he made that same gesture, to wipe his forehead, to push aside his hair? Was his face, too, streaked in blood? It seemed very probable. But how badly disfigured? He scrubbed a sleeve across his cheek, considering the point. Did he resemble something out of nightmares — ?

With a smothered oath, he pulled back from the stile. The lane was out, then. Even now at this time of night there was the risk of a chance car bowling by. And if it should happen to stop . . . A remote possibility, surely, but, in his present state, one he had no wish to counter with some flimsy, mocked-up excuse. A twist of grin.

'*Poaching, eh?*' . . .

'*Yes, sir, I was savaged by a rabbit* — '

For a few seconds he was tempted to make a wild detour; to swing away in the opposite direction and take himself off to Honeysett's. Simple enough to do, if long-winded, and the place had been

6

empty for nearly three months, boarded up since the death of the child after all that black-magic hanky-panky . . . there would be no problem getting in. The house stood alone, surrounded by trees, and he could come up on it through the graveyard. Once inside, it would be small trouble to wash and put himself to rights. In comfort.

He had already spun and taken his first step forward when memory jarred and made him pull up short. Hell! Of course, the house was no longer empty. The new rector had taken up residence a couple of weeks ago, just in time for the Christmas services. The new rector and some blasted crippled relative, or other — and God knew how many more like encumbrances. And probably all burning the midnight oil . . . He stood, gnawing his lip. His own place, then? And chance being seen by — No, wait! He had suddenly recalled where there was another water-tap set safely away from prying eyes. Handy, too, considering where he was heading. And, with his luck, probably fuggin frozen as well, he surmised gloomily. So? He'd just damned well have to unfreeze it, then, wouldn't he?

Keeping his head low, he ran along the hedgerow parallel to the lane beyond, halting once to rub as much of the stickiness from his fingers as he could on a tuft of crackling grass, and once to flatten himself beside some strands of barbed wire which were strung across his path. Momentarily he lay on his belly, listening, his cheek rasped by herbage that had itself seemingly frozen into wire, before wriggling forward under the barrier.

On the other side, another field, bare and still in the moonlight, two blind-looking farm cottages positioned far off on its tree-studded fringe. Small danger there. No sound, other than his heavy breathing and the cry of the wind, and, over to his right, away in the woods, the triple bark of a dog fox calling its mate.

Across the field, and another, past a row of darkened cottages, through a shave of wood, and he was rounding an old weed-filled pond, the water in it frozen now to a depth of several inches. Then he was climbing the crumbling, spike-crowned boundary wall of the Langdon estate, while trying desperately not to skewer his vitals. Once over, his tension eased. From now on in it would be plain sailing. He would clean himself up, maybe even take the knife from his pocket and wash it thoroughly — and then away home, with nothing more to fear between him and his goal but sweet, sodding damn-all.

Slackening his stride, he made his way towards the overgrown shrubberies, slipping smoothly and purposefully between the neglected rhododendrons with the air of one who had performed that particular feat many times before. The tool-shed, its lock already opened, stood on the far side of the bushes. It took but a moment to return the pickaxe and the spade to their racks, and then he was outside again, deftly snaking among the winter-bound shrubs as he headed towards the narrow lawn which ran the length of the badly-maintained rear driveway. Ice crackled beneath his feet and dead branches still lay where the autumn gales had felled them.

In summer, leafy boughs obscured the house at this point, but now it could be seen through the naked trees, a great pile of pale grey stone, whitened in the moonlight. At one a.m. it was silent, its windows blank, its inhabitants asleep. Even in daylight the house had a morbid atmosphere, a kind of brooding oppressiveness; at night it was downright sinister. Still, a bit of sinister silence, at the moment, he could take. He moved sharply across the drive and began walking to where a dilapidated wooden hut stood in shadow, an inky bulk dwarfed by the stricken elm behind it. The tree reared up, a huge dead girder against the sky. Icicles hung sharp as bayonets from the lower branches.

On reaching the wooden building, he rested his numbed hands on the doorposts on either side of him and fought an overwhelming urge to cough.

The hut in front of him had once been the old potting-shed, although precious little potting was carried on in there, nowadays, he thought wryly; the flower-beds, like the shrubberies, were fast rioting into ruin. The building itself looked as if a good push would cause it to collapse like a stack of cards, and already, before he entered, the remembered pungent smell of damp and decay was in his nostrils. The single oblong window, framing blackness, gazed at him like an unpleasantly watchful eye. Inside, he knew, was little of value; broken pots and seed-boxes, and a few mouldering rags and hanks of string and raffia, a couple of hurricane lamps, a long wooden bench, a kitchen chair — and a cold-water-tap over a stone sink in the corner. A quick sluice, and he would be on his way.

But the door was locked. He eyed the cheap padlock and iron clasp with a grim smile. It would take more than that to keep him out . . .

2

Spring. The Reverend Bevan Oake sniffed the mild air appreciatively. It had seemed a long time coming and the winter had been cruel, but, at last, the balm-and-blackthorn smell of spring. He could recognize the honeyed fragrance of broad beans in flower and, closer at hand, a sharper pungency that spoke of wild garlic. There were primroses on the banks, and violets under the hedges, and, high on the Downs, the small blue butterflies which were native to the chalk country were dancing in the sunshine. Sadly fewer now than when he was a lad, yet difficult, today, to feel sufficiently depressed by their dwindling numbers, with the wild cherry-tree boughs snowed under with blossom and a warm breeze ruffling the young wheat and, everywhere, gorse running across the scrubland in rivers of gold.

His eyes, grey and narrowed against the

glare, gazed about him.

Chatton Eastwood lay before him, tranquil in bright sunlight, an unspoiled village of clapboard and mellowed old rose brick set in a fold of the hills, halfway to nowhere. Above, the sheep-bitten sweep of the Downs; below, Chatton valley where the river wound clear and glittering under its weeping willows. His village now. His flock. And the tranquillity but a treacherous illusion.

With something resembling a sigh, Bevan Oake swung from the hill path, crossed the narrow strip of flower-studded grass between hedge and road, and started off down the main street to the village. Some people, when they spotted him coming, like biblical Levites crossed to the other side, others melted away before he reached them. No one spoke to him freely. Even after four months he was a stranger to them still, and he could number those who were his friends on the fingers of one hand: Theda and Lance Langdon, their father, Lawrence — and Cade Burrell. The latter, by his own admission, a loner who had little truck with the locals; and the Langdon family, owners of the Langdon estate and residents of the neighbourhood Big House and thus, by their very situation, already distanced from the villagers. He gave a crooked grin. Long live feudalism! His brother, Jonathan, had fared better. Perhaps being in a wheel-chair somehow conveyed its own ticket of entry.

'Good-morning, Mrs Bakewell.' Bevan raised his hand to the woman who was cleaning the window of a small general stores. She acknowledged his greeting with a faint nod of the head before scuttling inside, in her haste nearly treading upon a small child crouched on the step earnestly picking its nose.

For a moment he contemplated the closed door. Mrs Bakewell. One of those 'hysterical women' of whom his superiors had given warning? He would not himself have said so. The tight lips and gimlet eyes betokened someone firmly in con-trol. But did she expect him to ask questions? Questions that would have been, at best, embarrassing to answer?

Well, she could rest easy. What was past was past, and he had been advised to tread softly, to let sleeping dogs lie. Besides, the ringleaders had gone. As Jonathan succinctly put it: *Dead or fled.*

The coven, or circle or sect or whatever they had called it, had broken up. There was nothing like that in Chatton Eastwood now, or so he had been assured by those who wanted his services. Really, there had been nothing to it, just a gaggle of unbalanced, hysterical women — wise now to the error of their ways. He would have no trouble, no trouble at all. Bevan gave a crooked grin. That was just as well, because he wasn't certain if he'd recognize witchcraft if he saw it . . .

But what on earth made ordinary people turn to magic, and black magic at that? Something vital missing from their lives? Excitement? Or fear? . . . Placate the Dark God — ? He didn't pretend to understand. His brother insisted that it was a purely sexual thing; that all witch-craft malarkey was merely an excuse, a kind of *carte blanche* to indulge in

15

unorthodox sex, although Bevan wondered if, perhaps, it might have rather more to do with power. Power over people. Do as I say, or else! — Good luck, bad luck . . . at the flick of a finger.

He sometimes felt that much of mankind had crawled little further than the primeval bogs. Oh, it had its televisions and its up-to-date domestic appliances, its cars and its videos and its modern medicines, but under the surface there still lurked the ancient primitive beliefs. Scratch that surface and who knew what strange notions might be released, what devils let loose on reeling minds.

Still, Chatton Eastwood was quiet enough now, no rumblings of dark deeds after nightfall, no complaints of missing cocks or gutted goats, no sightings of naked dancers among the trees. Probably because it had been cold enough these past few months to freeze even the most sturdy witch into stark immobility, thought Bevan with sardonic humour. He would just have to wait and see what the thaw might bring.

'Admiring the décor, Mr Oake?'

A voice like honey running over a file.

Bevan jumped several inches and grinned inanely back at the face smiling at him from the window glass. Elise Walters. He rounded. Eyes that were green and gold and speckled with sunlight, and as bright as the morning. Ghost eyes. Julie's eyes. Somewhere, a knife turned.

'I was — ' He cleared his throat. Dark hair whipped up and whirled around her crown in what Bevan mentally called an 'onion' knot. Julie, too, had often worn her hair like that, but there the resemblance ended. His wife had always appeared neat as a new pin, whereas this girl looked as if she might recently have been dragged through a hedge backwards. Wisps of hair drifted untidily about her forehead and one thick tendril had tugged free from its anchorage and was curling over her left shoulder. His fingers itched to pin it back. He cleared his throat again. 'I was wondering whether to get some stamps,' he said primly.

'Big decision.' The pale eyes danced at

17

him. 'I'd hate to watch you make the buy of the season . . . You've been staring in at that window for the past five minutes, and I couldn't believe it was Mrs Bakewell's tarts that'd grabbed you.'

Brazen, Mrs Pawcett, his housekeeper, said. And no better than she should be . . . would make her poor mother turn in her grave. Mrs Pawcett didn't like her.

Mrs Pawcett, as Bevan had found out by fast elimination, didn't like anyone.

Elise gave him her wide smile. 'Cheer up. You look as if someone's clobbered your canary — '

'I've just been to the Goodes,' replied Bevan, in what emerged as a censorious tone, and watched the light fade in the brilliant eyes.

'Oh, grief, I'm sorry.' She stared at him, appalled by her blunder. 'I'd forgotten. Those poor parents — poor little Robin . . . '

He wiped the sweating palm of his hand against his trouser-leg.

'Thank you for arranging last Sunday's flowers, Elise, and at such short notice.'

'That was okay. Any time — ' The wide

generous smile encompassed him again, as warmly as it apparently enfolded everyone else. 'I must rush, Mr Oake. The Langdons have allowed me an hour off — ' She bent to scoop the child up from the step and set it astride her hip. 'Come along, Susie, I'll take you home to your mother . . . ' A swift nuzzle on the side of the tiny bare neck. And she was gone.

Bevan crossed the road in her wake to where a low brick wall jutted out from the Jobbers' Arms. Arthur Sullivan was lolling against the brickwork there with a carroty-haired crony from one of the neighbouring villages. Both were absorbed in watching the antics of something imprisoned in a small bottle.

'A pint it dies in the next half hour — '

'It won't.'

'Betcha — '

The two heads jerked up as Bevan's shadow fell over them.

Arthur Sullivan scowled mightily. His low brow and undershot jaw had once moved Jonathan to dub him the original Neanderthal man, a description now indelibly printed on the rector's mind for all time.

'Good-day to you both,' Bevan said, pausing determinedly to talk.

'Lo, Rector.' Arthur shuffled his feet, bereft of anything further to say.

The stoppered bottle beside him contained a large fly, lying on its back. Dead, so Bevan thought until he noticed the legs still weakly waving.

'Nice morning,' he remarked.

'Uh, huh.' Arthur's grunt added little brilliance to the conversation, and silence stretched between them like overstrained elastic.

Catching Bevan's eye, the tongue-tied companion with the flaming thatch suddenly uttered a strangled bray and bolted away from them, racing diagonally across the courtyard of the Jobbers' Arms until he vanished around the corner.

'Sorry I frightened him,' said Bevan, with a tinge of irony.

'S'all right,' mumbled Arthur. He scratched the bristles on his chin.

Bevan's eyes strayed again to the fly. It was still buzzing feebly on its back, its wings driving it round and round the bottom of the bottle. Rather a grisly way to expire, but Bevan lacked the moral courage to protest. There were worse sins than torturing flies. A small bitter smile quivered at the corners of his mouth. His forte these days seemed to be an ability to turn a blind eye . . .

By his side, Arthur hawked and spat glutinously.

'Did you want summat, Rector?'

Bevan considered. 'No.'

'I expect you'm in a hurry to be off, then?'

'No.'

Arthur stood glumly pulling at his ear. Then brightened. His little eyes took on a cunning glint.

'I gotta take a leak,' he said, and shuffled off towards a disinfectant-reeking building at the side of the Jobbers' Arms.

Defeated, Bevan continued on his way along the road. Neat gardens and swept driveways; plump cats on sunny steps; babies in prams and pretty toddlers on lawns; a beach-ball flying to his feet to be gently tossed back again. Nothing here of the powers of darkness. The witches, if witches there were, must be safely at home, polishing their broomsticks.

Near the village duckpond — called by the villagers, with characteristic flair, the Pond — he paused beside some railings. The school yard, and little girls chanting and swinging in and out of a turning rope.

'*Mercy, Mercy Goodbright,*
Fly away, and so . . . Goodnight.'

Fleetingly, he wondered about the unknown Mercy Goodbright. Some local legend, maybe? He'd have to inquire. He'd never heard that particular rhyme before. And what had she done to bring her fame — or notoriety?

One of the little girls, long fair hair and a wide smile, waved a benign hand at him. Her charity cost her dear, for the upward swing of the rope caught her arm, throwing her off balance, so that she tripped and fell in an ignominious heap.

Bevan turned away. Never wise to witness humiliation.

He and Julie had never had children, and after the accident he had been glad.

A child of that first year of their marriage would now have been — what? Nine. Old enough to miss a mother, not old enough to cope without her. The same age, roughly, as those little girls, skipping. The same age as Robin Goode, whose life had been so tragically cut short by a hit-and-run driver the previous day. Mown down and left dead in a ditch along the Hatchins road, his head pillowed on a rock and his crumpled bicycle beside him.

Bevan had been to see the Goodes that morning, in their neat farmhouse high on the hill. Both parents had been stunned. Grief-stricken. Riddled with guilt. Bevan understood the corrosive effect of that. 'If we hadn't bought him that new bike — ' they kept saying, over and over again. 'If we hadn't bought him that bike — '

Not an only child, Robin, but the only child still at home. There was an older boy, away somewhere in the city. Hopefully, now he would come back . . .

Two young children in the churchyard, then, within seven months, and the death of that first child laid fairly and squarely at his predecessor's door. Small wonder that the village was dour and suspicious. Bevan had heard the rumours; some kind of exorcism which had gone horrifyingly wrong — and the Reverend Honeysett carried off, raving like a lunatic. The poor fellow had since committed suicide; thrown himself under a train, so it was said, and, with indecent haste, Bevan had been offered, and accepted, Chatton Eastwood.

To Bevan the appointment had been the answer to a prayer. He could not have remained much longer where he was, not after the death of Julie. Not with the memory of her engraved on every brick and stone. She had been the first girl he had ever loved, and he'd never loved another. Even after eighteen months he still missed her more than was passively bearable. He glanced about him. But here he might at last begin to grope his way forward. It was just that sometimes — a twist of a head . . . the lilt of a voice . . . the ghost of a smile . . .

And there was, of course, Jonathan. He pictured his brother's face, the dark good looks thinned by months of pain to something that was almost saturnine; the caustic tongue dipped in a deeper acid. The house was ideal for Jonathan.

Leaving the outskirts of the village behind, Bevan started on his way down the hill towards the lower bridge — Frognalls — a route not much used since the road through the Frognalls estate had been closed. Quicker now to go by the upper crossing, via the Hatchins road. He moved briskly, used to walking. He no longer possessed a car, loathed travelling in one, although the phobia would, hopefully, burn itself out in time. Jonathan, however, had no such lingering fears. And no guilt.

Funny how we fashion our own destinies, thought Bevan. The accident had been his fault. Oh, not directly. Everyone had said that he was not to blame, that the other driver was drunk and speeding along on the wrong side of the road; that Bevan was entirely guiltless. No matter that he had been the one in the driver's seat . . .

Been there by his own insistence!

That night, as usual, Jonathan had had too much to drink; not enough to be reeling, but enough to be, well — merry. He, Bevan, had demanded that he should be the one to drive.

The echo of his supercilious tone was with him still.

And so, pottering along at regulation speed, stone-cold sober at the wheel, Bevan had driven the car which had killed his wife and put his brother into a wheelchair.

And if he had not?

Ah, there was the rub. Who could tell? Perhaps if he had relinquished the wheel to Jonathan, to cutting-tongued, devil-may-care, rash Jonathan, who had always driven too fast and too recklessly, their car might never have crossed the path of that other, might have been minutes gone . . . Useless, now, to consider the odds.

He rested his arms on the parapet of the bridge and stared down at the purling water. The river Chatton, clear and shallow, and glittering here and there like tears. He could see the pebbles quite plainly at the bottom, and shoals of tiny fish that freckled the sunlit water. In places there grew great patches of vivid emerald-green waterweed, combed out by the current into mermaids' hair.

Once, this gentle river had been a savage waterway, rising in times of flood to thunder underneath its bridges, battering so fiercely at the pilings that, sometime during the seventeen hundreds, the bridge at this particular spot had been swept away. The present structure, sturdy, functional and built of darkened bricks which had been arrowed into cutwaters at the base and pierced through at the — then-normal high water-level to break the fury of the current, had been a gift from the Frognalls estate. The foresight which had provided those safety features had also been unnecessary; successive years of booming industries making heavy use of the Chatton, and various alterations to its course, had caused the level of the water to drop drastically. Each year the river seemed to shrink a little. Soon, a good-sized plank would cross it.

Bevan raised his head and stared to where a stone wall, unpleasantly guarded

27

along the top with coils of barbed wire, rose blank upon the far side of the bridge. Dangerous, if one were speeding down the hill and failed to turn sharply left or right. A section of more brightly coloured stonework showed where the entrance had once been and where, before ownership of the estate had changed hands, the old road had once run through. Already at this T-junction there had been two accidents.

To his left, the land rose again steeply until it was crowned by a ruined watchtower brooding black and jagged against the sky. When unlocked — the key, for some reason or other, was kept at the rectory — it gave a fine view of the surrounding countryside. Beyond the tower the ground fell away in a sheer chalk cliff to the rocks below. Impossible to climb.

Bevan presumed the edifice had once kept guard over Frognalls, alerting those there to any impending attack from land, or from the then navigable waterway. Now, only the sheep, cropping the short grass of the hillside, disturbed the peace.

Taking a deep breath of the blackthorn-scented air, he straightened his back and set off again across the bridge and, wheeling sharply to his right, along the righthand curve of the lane beside the high, discouraging stone wall. On his other hand, hedges and tall trees and, round the second bend, a rutted cart-track which led to a dilapidated slate-loose cottage — the insalubrious abode of Amos White and his family.

3

Amos was the village blight; a dirty, evil-minded, cantankerous old man who, if Bevan were to believe all accounts, treated his children abominably. Bevan himself had seen the man but twice, once when the fellow had arrived to receive the Langdons' traditional Christmas dole, and once staggering home from the Jobbers' Arms, from which he'd since been banned for following up his Happy New Year with a Happy New brick through the said public house's window. On all other occasions Amos had refused to meet him, remaining firmly behind his locked door while his whey-faced daughter had indicated dumbly from the window that Bevan should take himself away. However, Amos had now disappeared; had walked out a couple of nights ago and not come back, so his son, Seth, had told Mrs Pawcett, who'd promptly informed everybody else. And a good thing, too, was the general consensus of opinion. But a couple of nights ago there had also been a burglary at the Langdons' —

Bevan frowned at the tar-boarded cottage in its tangled garden. Difficult to tell where wilderness left off and path began. He could see Seth through the window of an open-doored outhouse attached to the main building. His head was bent and he was working at something on a bench. Three boys with chickenpox-scabbed faces were leaning on the sill outside, jeering. The Burns brothers. Bevan pushed at the gate.

'Shouldn't go in there, Mister,' shouted one of the youngsters as Bevan strolled up the would-be path towards them. 'Whitey stinks like a polecat.'

Maybe it was true, a certain stench did seem to be greeting Bevan on the wind. Without a word he pointed with an arm towards the gate and the boys slunk off through it, only to turn outside and drape themselves over the top bar.

Bevan stuck his head through the doorway.

'Hello, Seth. May I come in?' Without waiting for an answer he stepped over the threshold.

Seth White looked up startled.

'Mr Oake.'

The deep-set eyes that stared back at Bevan were clear and greyish-green, like the sea, and possibly as changeable. They had small pale flecks in them, like ice.

'It's a lovely day.'

'Yes, Mr Oake.' Wary. Probably thinks I'm going to ask him why he doesn't attend church, thought Bevan wryly, studying the thin frame and countenance before him. It was not an easy face.

Seth White was a slight, hatchet-featured youth of about seventeen — twenty years younger than Bevan — wearing, at that moment, dirty jeans and plimsolls, and a torn denim jacket from which his knobbly wrists protruded by several inches. His dark hair, hacked roughly in the style of an Amazonian Indian, was tousled and in need of a good wash.

'Their taunting doesn't trouble you?' asked Bevan, indicating the cat-calling boys.

'No. Why should it?' replied Seth in a placid tone. 'Makes Amos as sick as a parrot, though.' He gave a grin in which the devil showed through.

'I hear they were tormenting Kathie last week, down by the river.'

'That's right.' For the first time, Seth scowled. 'That makes me see red, right enough; it upsets her. Those three — and Robin Goode.'

'I heard he was the ringleader. I was going to have a word with him, but . . .' Bevan's voice trailed away.

'Won't be doing it no more, will he?'

Bevan stared at the ice-chip eyes. It was fortunate that the lad couldn't drive a car or folk might have been forced to wonder . . . He peered down at the contraption of thongs and spherical weights under the boy's hand.

'What are you doing?' he asked curiously.

Seth tapped the articles on the bench. 'Making myself another rabbit-catcher. I had a fine one, but I seem to have lost it somewhere.' His voice was deep, with an abrasive edge. 'A rabbit comes in handy for the pot . . . But so does most anything else, for that matter — ' He gave a smile of mingled mischief and bravado. 'Squirrel, pigeon, cat — ' Spinning the contraption he had made, he let it fly, out through the open door of the outhouse and along the path where it wrapped itself viciously round a broken post.

'*Bolas*,' said Bevan. Seth looked at him with such startled eyes that the rector was forced to elaborate.

'In South America they call it *bolas* — the cowboys there use it instead of a lasso.'

'Is that so?'

Bevan wondered if he had really caught that faint tinge of mockery in the young voice, or if it had been a product of his imagination.

He said: 'You're on your own?'

'No.' Seth jerked his head towards an inner door.

'There's Kathie.'

'Yes, I know. But Amos — your father — hasn't returned?' Bevan paused. 'You've no idea where he could be?'

'No. Walked out and didn't walk back

— and good riddance, I say.' There was a venomous undercut to the words. He stepped past Bevan and down the path outside to reclaim his rabbit-catcher, and then placed it reverently upon the bench. He gave it a little pat of approval with his hand before moving across the room to open the inner door which led to the kitchen.

Bevan had the feeling he was being dismissed.

He said quickly: 'A couple of nights ago, wasn't it, when your father sloped off?' He stole a sideways glance at his companion. 'The same time as Langdons had their burglary. You don't think Amos could have had anything to do with that?'

Seth shrugged.

'No,' mused Bevan. 'Tapestries. That's a pretty narrow field, I should say.'

Again Seth shrugged.

The notion was ridiculous, thought Bevan. The old man was none too bright, and would have had no idea how to dispose of antiques. If he were going to steal something it would have been something easily portable, and readily saleable; a radio, clock, or a piece of silver, not some great galumphing mediaeval tapestry. He had pinched things right enough, from all accounts, but in a smaller league; the odd pheasant here and there, somebody's chickens, things from an unlocked car —

Bevan frowned. 'Do you need any help?'

'No,' said Seth uncompromisingly. 'We can manage.'

But not very well, surmised Bevan, glancing in through the kitchen door; the place was a shambles, dirty dishes piled high in the sink, filth on the floor, and over all the smell of unwashed bodies and unclean clothes. Kathie didn't appear to be capable of much. She was curled in a chair by the unlit fire, staring into space.

'Hello, Kathie,' called Bevan, moving forward.

The girl was younger than her brother by about two years, and as thin and dark and as sharp-featured as he was. Her unkempt hair hung in rats'-tails to her waist.

Maybe, if Amos really had gone,

someone could take the pair in hand. Mrs Pawcett? Bevan flinched inwardly. Mrs Pawcett's abrasive tongue and harsh manner would hardly be the balm required here. The White kids needed warmth, care, affection — someone kind and generous like . . . He paused in thought. Like Elise Walters. He had no doubt that Elise would sweep them under her wing and put the cottage to rights in a twinkling. Probably fatten up the pair of them, too. He glanced at the girl's thin shoulders. For several minutes he tried to provoke some response from her, but failed utterly. To all his overtures she said nothing, just continued to stare at him with great, strange eyes that reminded him of some wild animal.

After a while, he said: 'I'm going to send you some help.'

'We don't want help,' returned Seth, defiantly.

'This help you'll want,' smiled Bevan. He stepped to the door. 'May I cut across your back garden? I want to see Cade Burrell, and there's a path on the other side of your property which will take me through to Langdons'.' Cade Burrell both lived and worked on the Langdon estate.

Seth nodded without speaking and trailed Bevan outside. The three Burns boys were still at the gate but had now been joined by their elder sister, Peggy, who had obviously been sent to retrieve them. The girl, pretty and full-breasted, tossed her head when she saw Seth and grabbed the two smaller brothers on either hand.

'Come on,' she said peremptorily. 'Home.' She swept them along with her, glancing back over a raised shoulder to see if Seth were watching her. He was. He was unable to take his eyes off her . . .

Bevan frowned. He wasn't sure that he cared much for Peggy Burns; a cold-hearted, teasing little baggage. He could see that Seth did not share his view: Seth was all but drooling. Easy lad, sighed Bevan inwardly, you don't want to tangle there, not with someone as self-centered as Peggy. In his opinion, Seth needed a girl with a little more warmth and a lot more kindness, someone strong enough to counter Amos's hard and unloving hand. Again his thoughts flew to Elise, and he grinned wryly at his silent monologue. 'I have a little job for you, Elise. Just trot along to the Whites' place, will you? and scrub the stinking hovel from top to bottom. Then, as a favour to me, pop into the lad's bed and give him a good time — '

He chortled harshly to himself as he swung away across the little tufted field towards the woods. he could just imagine the fair, warm Elise's reaction to that!

A fair, warm fist knuckling his mouth . . .

The midday sun dazzled his eyes. Among the trees it would be cool and quiet, the ground traced with an embroidery of light and shade. He quickened his pace, eager to step into shadow, and, going from bright sunlight to dimness, almost knotted himself into a vast, elaborate concoction of string which was woven between two trees. Disentangling his arms, he stepped back and stared at the phenomenon. It appeared to be some kind of net made up of intricately woven patterns which looked for all the world like some giant cat's-cradle. Some form of trap? He pondered on the animal it could have been set to catch, and could think of nothing likely. Cade Burrell was a woodsman, he'd ask him.

But Cade laughed at the question.

'Nothing you're ever going to see, Bevan . . . It's laid for a ghost.'

He was even more amused by Bevan's patent disbelief.

'It's so, I'm telling you. They're a primitive lot around here. You're out in the boonies now, mate, not among nice cosy council flats in the big city. Someone's set a trap to catch a ghost. The web's been put there to prevent some restless spirit walking in on them.'

'You're not serious?'

'As a judge.'

'This is the twentieth century — '

'Not around here, mate. Here, you're stuck somewhere in the Dark Ages. Mind you, I had thought that particular little trick had died out years ago. I can remember my granny telling me about it, though . . . ' He flicked a glance at Bevan. 'You'll find the contraption has probably been strung between the weaver's pad and the boneyard.' He grinned. 'Where'd you find it?'

'At the north end of Drearden's Wood.'

Cade's eyes flickered momentarily. There was a pause that lasted no longer than a catch of breath before he said: 'You work it out then, Bevan old son; a nice little riddle for your long lonely evenings.'

Bevan sat on a tree-stump watching the strong brown hands steady at their task. Cade was constructing a five-barred gate, one roughly four feet high and ten wide, out of seasoned oak.

'That's some fine timber,' remarked Bevan at last.

'Aye. None of your usual rubbish. Old man Langdon wants the best. Fastened with oak pegs instead of iron bolts this will last a hundred years.' A gleam of smile. 'See the old man out, this will, and his son after him.'

'Expensive, though, surely?'

'Aye.' The hands went about their work deftly.

'Making things that last usually is.'

'There's a lot needs doing on the estate.'

Cade nodded. 'And me the only chap to do it. Full time, that is. And while I'm doing this I can't be after doing anything else, like; although there's a load of cord-wood on the lorry as needs delivering . . . But the old man says he don't fancy any of that factory trash.' He smoothed his hand along the crosspiece fondly. 'For the ten-acre, this is.'

It beat Bevan. During the time it took Cade to make that gate he could equally well have been mending the barn, tiling the roof, replacing a few doors, planting something — or hanging a score of factory-bought gates that would have served the same purpose . . .

'It's what the old man wants,' said Cade, his dark eyes on the frown between Bevan's brows. 'With the young one, of course, things might be different.'

'Have they had any joy yet over their robbery?'

'No, and not likely to, I'd say. Stuff'll be long gone by now. Probably out of the country. Miss Theda says it was the only decent tackle left in the place.'

'Been selling, haven't they?'

'That's right. The place is falling apart — Needs a mint spent on it.'

Bevan glanced across at his companion. 'Amos White. He works with you sometimes, doesn't he?'

'Rarely,' said Cade with dry humour. 'He manages a bit of casual labour on the estate from time to time. But he's not been here in ages. In winter he's like the hedgehog. Tanks up and then hibernates.' He gave a grunt. 'Down in that ramshackle old cottage of his.'

'You don't think his disappearance could have anything to do with the Langdon robbery?'

'I doubt it,' replied Cade. 'Old Amos wouldn't have the wit to tell a tapestry from a teatowel. Pheasants are more in his line.'

'That's what I thought.'

Cade grinned. 'And it's hardly a disappearance, mate, is it? He's only been gone for two days, so Seth says. And he's done that before. If he's living rough it won't hurt him, weather's mild enough. Man's probably dead drunk in a ditch somewhere. You could ask Arthur

Sullivan if he has any idea where the old chap might be — if Seth wants his father back home that quickly, that is — He and Amos are buddies.'

'I thought, while Amos is missing, it might be a good plan to ask Elise Walters to look in on his children. They need some help. The cottage is in a mess, and I think Seth and Kathie could do with a benevolent hand. Elise would be very good for them.'

'Aye. Very medicinal,' replied Cade dryly.

'You think it would be a good idea, then?'

'I don't see why not . . . if Elise is willing.'

'I'll step in and have a word with her, then, on my way home.' Bevan looked relieved. Seth and Kathie White were heavy on his conscience.

4

Elise Walters paused, her hand on the sagging gate before her. What on earth was she doing there? The Reverend Oake's bidding? A small smile curved her mouth as she turned to watch the Land-Rover, which had deposited her on the sun-scented grass outside Amos White's cottage, bump its way back along the cart-track. Through the open rear of the vehicle she could see the two moon-gold heads shining, side by side, pale as the primroses that starred the verges to left and right of her. Lance Langdon was driving, his concentration wholly taken up by the winter-carved ruts in front of him, but his sister Theda raised an arm in one last wave of farewell before they swung from sight. Somehow, a strangely appropriate gesture, thought Elise grimly, eyeing the unprepossessing homestead ahead.

Isolated, ugly, falling into disrepair, the

building was such that even the sunshine could not make it look other than infinitely depressing. But she was not there to ponder upon the place's lack of charm, was she? Nor was she there at Bevan Oake's special request, no matter what that reverend gentleman might think. She would have come anyway, to see Seth and Kathie; they were, after all, kin. But the rector could congratulate his conscience as he chose . . .

Kicking aside a rusted tin, Elise trod firmly forward across the matted grass.

Seth she found crouched under a cherry tree on the far side of the cottage. Sleeves rolled above his elbows and shirt open to the waist, he appeared to be dismembering an old box-sofa.

'Good-morning, Seth,' she beamed as she reached him.

Seth looked up from what he was doing, then straightened his back.

'Hello, Elise.' If he were surprised to see her, he failed to show it. 'I think it should be 'good-afternoon', it's after midday.' He squinted up at the sun enmeshed high among the flowering cherry boughs before turning to grin at her. 'What brings you this way?'

She set down the carrier-bag she had been holding and her mouth curved back at him. 'The hope that Amos is out. I heard he'd gone away.'

'You heard right, then.'

'May I come in?'

'You're in, aren't you?' The warmth of his smile smoothed the roughness from the words.

'The rector said you might need some help,' she said, as Seth returned his attention to his task.

'Rector's an interfering old windbag.'

'He means well.'

'He does?' Seth gave one end of the wooden sofa a vicious clout with his hammer. As if in sympathy, the cherry tree released a sudden cloud of petals which drifted down like snowflakes upon the two dark heads below. 'Then he wants to keep his snout out of things that don't concern him.'

'I think he felt you and Kathie were his concern,' remarked Elise gently.

Seth merely scowled.

Elise stepped closer to him. He was no taller than she was and, weight for weight, she could probably give him a pound or two.

'Then you want me to go?'

His head jerked up at that. 'No, of course I don't want you to go.' He stared at her. 'You've only just come. How did you get here, anyway? With one of the Langdons? I thought I heard their Land-Rover.'

She nodded. 'Theda and Lance are off on a pigeon-shoot. They were kind enough to run me here after I'd finished work. Today was one of my mornings at the House.'

'I do remember,' he said with faint irony.

'Yes — ' She flashed him a puzzled glance from under her lashes. 'We've missed you up at the House, Seth.'

'I'm sure.'

'Truly.'

He gave a sardonic little smile. 'Doubtless the Langdons were able to overcome their heartache.'

'I wasn't talking about the Langdons — '

She touched his bare arm and felt a shiver run along his flesh. 'Why didn't you come back? I thought you enjoyed working on the estate. You haven't been near since Christmas.'

'Amos had me otherwise occupied.'

'I see.'

'I doubt it.' Again the sardonic smile. He raised his head once more and chanced a good eyeful of her. She had the power to make his stomach churn and, recognizing the familiar surge of heat in him, he forced himself to concentrate upon his hammering.

Elise watched the agitated movement of his hands for several seconds, then said lightly: 'What are you making? A coffin?'

'What?' He flung her a startled look.

'Your fancy woodwork.' She prodded the disintegrating sofa with her toe. 'What is it going to be?'

'Oh, that?' He glanced down. 'A rabbit-hutch, eventually.'

'Lucky rabbit — '

But Seth was not listening. He had raised his eyes to the level of the second button on the low-cut bodice of her dress and there had stuck, hypnotized by the tantalizing swell beneath the taut fabric. Someone, somewhere — and more informed than he was — had once told him that, apart from such outer sops to decency, Elise Walters went bare. Was it true? If he undid those two straining upper buttons, would her breasts round out to fill his hands, soft and warm as a pair of nestling doves? His eyes slipped slowly downwards. She had a neat waist and generous hips, a seductive curve that led his inflamed imagination to run exploratory fingers up her skirt. If — He caught at his runaway thoughts and felt his face grow hot.

He shot a half-shamed glance towards Elise. She was staring at him with a mocking smile just staining the corners of her lips, and he wondered if it were possible that she had read his mind. He hoped not. But with Elise one always wondered . . . In her white dress, with the petals confetti in her long, loose hair, she looked like a bride.

'Come back,' said Elise. 'Wherever you are.' She slid the hammer from his hand

and dropped it to the grass. 'That can wait a while, can't it?'

He nodded speechlessly, all too conscious of her nearness.

'Is Kathie all right?' she demanded.

'She is now,' Seth replied cryptically. He bobbed his head towards the house. 'Want to sleep — I mean, step — in and see her?'

'That was the general idea.' Elise picked up the bag which had been standing beside her, and threw him a wide grin. 'I've brought my brush and apron.'

The Reverend Oake had not exaggerated; the place was like a pigsty, if one didn't object to insulting pigs, thought Elise. A good scrub down certainly wouldn't come amiss. And it smelled of damp.

'It's a bit of a mess,' said Seth apologetically.

His sister, who was sitting by the unlit kitchen fire, turned to face Elise with eyes that were wide and wild, and unexpectedly hostile, before once more lapsing into her vacant contemplation of the empty grate.

'We'll have that lit, for a start,' decided Elise. 'The place is like a morgue in here, for all the sunshine outside. And do you realize that we've got to put bread on that disgusting table?'

'Been working on it, haven't I?' said Seth defensively.

'What with? A bow-saw?' She swept away the debris and wiped down the surface. Then swung abruptly to Seth again. 'Have you eaten?'

'Not so that you'd notice.' He gave a slight smile. 'But there's a rabbit in the outhouse, when we get around to it.'

Elise got around to it straight away and, while they were waiting for the food to cook, she attacked the worst of the filthy floor, and the pile of dirty dishes. In fact, for the rest of the day, she did little else other than wield a selection of cleaning materials, most of which she'd had the foresight to bring with her, for there was nothing in the cottage. Amos must have enjoyed his squalor. Leaning her arms on the sun-warmed window-sill for a moment towards late evening, she pictured his return; the scene would not be without a certain acrid humour.

'When do you expect him to come back?' she called to Seth over her shoulder. 'Amos, I mean.'

He walked across the room to stand beside her. She was tinglingly alive to the intimate, faint animal warmth that came from him.

'God knows.'

'Well, hazard an educated guess. One week? Two? How long does he usually go walkabout?'

Seth shrugged.

'Oh, for heaven's sake, Seth!' She eyed him in mock despair. 'You're not being much help. You must have some idea. You know his habits . . . Till his money runs out, say?'

Seth leaned his arms on the sill beside her and turned towards her, feeling her soft hair brush against his cheek. It smelled of green apple shampoo and sunshine.

He said, very quietly: 'I don't believe he's coming back.'

'But — '

'Don't ask me why. I just don't, that's

all. This time I think he's gone for good . . . We're free of him, Elise.' His eyes ranged past her and through the window, following the course of the weed-tangled path. 'It takes some getting used to.'

'I can see that,' rejoined Elise with a trace of irony, recalling the midden she had just been called upon to clear. True, Seth had assisted her, doing her bidding with an almost pathetic eagerness, but Kathie would have been handier with a hoe. Pleading a headache, the girl had now taken herself off to bed. Elise sighed.

'Tired?' Seth's eyes came back to rest on hers.

She produced a faint smile. 'What do you think?'

'I had hoped — not.' The slight pause and emphasis gave the words a more suggestive ring than he had, perhaps, intended. Elise's eyes flickered. She was not inexperienced, nor was she made of wood, and she recognized his need of her, knew the ache which had been growing steadily within him with every hour that passed. He wanted her, now quite desperately. And she was beginning to feel an answering kindling in her blood. If she were going to go, it would have to be now.

Even as she turned from the window, his arms came out and around her, crushing her to his chest. Her body melted willingly against him.

'Stay,' he said hoarsely, in a voice that she could not identify as his own. 'Stay with me, Elise . . . ' His lips were on her hair, her mouth, her throat; his fingers tugging insistently at the fastenings of her dress, powered by a desire too strong for either skill or subtlety.

'Where else?' she whispered, feeling the responding pounding of her flesh as her own arms tightened on him and she gave herself up to his driving need to take her. Where else, indeed, my dear . . . ?

★   ★   ★

The sun fingered the tossed back coverlet of the big bed, stroking warmth across the tangle of bare arms and legs that sprawled there. Creeping slowly upwards it flung at last a brilliant hand across the sleepers' eyes and almost simultaneously they woke. Or one, by some vague twitch of movement, woke the other. Immediately they turned to smile into each other's eyes, surprised by the flame that had been lit between them. Surprised by a bond of mutual joy.

Strange how lust could turn to tenderness, and passion to love, mused Elise, watching the play of light on her companion's pale skin.

Seth raised himself on one elbow to look at her.

'Beautiful,' he sighed, in one word encompassing the naked girl beside him, the morning, and the past incredible night. 'I've been dreaming of — that — for ages. Had such fantasies . . . God, you'd not believe.' He traced his fingers down her cheek. 'But . . . even more mind-blowing in the flesh!'

Elise caught his hand and bit it. 'Rather too much in the flesh, bucko,' she said, feeling herself to be stiff and sore. 'And if that's the usual tenor of your dreams, shame on you.'

'Shame on *you*,' he grinned, his eyes ranging along the uncovered lovely length of her. 'Seducing this innocent boy.'

'Is that what you'll tell everybody?'

'It's what they'll believe.'

'Of course.' She grinned happily back at him. 'Do you mind?'

'Not if you don't.' He glanced towards the window. 'Sun's well up.'

'Lord,' she groaned. And closed her eyes. 'Work. I feel as if I've been run over by a ten-ton truck.'

'You've had a long, hard night,' he said dryly.

Her eyes flashed open at that and she gave a curve of smile. 'Oh, don't let your hackles rise, old son, you didn't do so badly. What you lacked in skill you made up in enthusiasm.'

Seth lay back against the pillow and stretched his arms to either side in a blithe gesture of luxurious abandonment. 'And practice, they say, makes perfect. So come here, my gorgeous girl, and let's christen this lovely morning.'

She looked at him laughingly. 'Do you realize that it's ten o'clock, and I'm supposed to be at the Langdons?'

'Tell them to stuff their job. You'll have

your work cut out with me — ' His arm
came out and clinched around her waist.
'First bedded and then wedded . . . '

'Seth! I must *go.*'

'If you insist. But first — ' He pulled
her, struggling, across his naked thighs
and began to caress her with his hand.

'Devil,' she said, from between her
teeth.

'That's right,' he grinned. 'You've got it
in one. Devil's spawn, Amos called me.
Old Horny . . . And don't you love it!'

She stopped fighting to get free and
gave herself up to the fierce pleasure of
his love-making. Rough and impetuous as
it was, it was none the less being speedily
honed for her delight as well as for his
own. And love went where it pleased.
Odd, the corners in which it blossomed.
Odd, and unexpected . . . She arched
suddenly under his hand.

'Now,' she gasped urgently. 'Seth.
Now.' And he took her; spinning her with
him deeper and deeper into the reeling
light, and then beyond, mindless, without
will, at one with the crackling stars, until,
burned out, she collapsed into a sleep of

sated exhaustion . . .

Somewhere, outside the window, a bird was singing. She could hear it, and, nearer at hand, Seth's voice, drifting in and out of her consciousness. She kept her eyes shut. Then, abruptly, became sensible to what he was saying, his mouth against her hair.

Pulling hurriedly away from him, she sat back on her heels and gazed at him with incredulous eyes.

'Marry you! You're asking me to marry you?'

His mouth quirked at the corners. 'Why so strange? I haven't got two heads. And all my parts are in working order. Besides, I love you. If I'm to believe you, and my senses, you love me; so surely — '

'What's that got to do with it?'

Again that quirk of smile. 'I thought it would be the proper thing to do. After all, you've been bouncing around in my bed.' He flicked her a grin. 'You've said yourself, I'm a lusty lad. There could be — consequences.' He'd like that. To give her his baby. To set his visible brand on her.

'Oh, that.' She shrugged it off, although for the first time in a sexual encounter she had taken no precautions. And Seth clearly hadn't. However, that was small matter nowadays.

'No,' he frowned gently, reading her mind, 'I shouldn't like you to take that way out.'

'Well, we'll cross that doubtful bridge if we come to it, in the meantime — '

'In the meantime, I see the Reverend Oake.' He could be as stubborn as she was.

She wanted to laugh, except she felt that that might hurt him. Scowling at her from under his tousled thatch of hair he looked even younger than his years.

'Love,' she said, 'I'm not going to fly away, ring or no ring. And marriage does seem — well, rather . . . excessive. Seth, I'm a good bit older than you are.'

'Eight years. I can do my sums.'

'It's a big difference when you're only seventeen.'

'Eighteen next month.' His mouth curved. 'And at this rate you'll age me fast.'

'And another thing. Suppose Amos came back?'

'He's not coming back. He's dead, can't you feel it, a lightening of the air? He's lying in a ditch somewhere, or has fallen under a car.'

'Oh, I do love a cheerful man.'

'So, any more arguments to shoot down?' He picked up a lock of her hair and draped it across the rosy points of her breasts. 'You're a rare one for wasting play time.'

She laughed. 'My love, I'll sleep with you, eat with you, work with you — '

'A very neat sense of the priorities of things — '

'But we don't need more — ' She sent him a brief flashing glance. 'Seth, don't you know what they say about me?' Her right hand traced a moth-like course across his thin back, feeling again the savage scars she'd noticed when he'd removed his shirt. She had not asked him about them; if he wanted to discuss them, then he'd do so. She was content to wait. 'And some of what they say is true. Not all, but some. Enough, anyhow.'

61

'So?'

'I'm trying to point out that I've had rather more experience than you have. More . . . 'partners' anyhow — '

'God, do you think I care?' He grimaced. 'Compared with some of the unsavoury things I've done, your list's pure as the driven snow . . . '

'I doubt that.' She glanced sideways at him. 'You must have heard talk.'

'Some.'

'What, exactly?'

He looked her in the eye. 'That you're easy.'

Easy, silky, seductive Elise. He felt a tremor deep within him and wondered why at the moment the whole of his waking thoughts — and a good many of his sleeping ones — appeared to be geared to sex; for months he'd been obsessed with little else. The ways, and the means — coupled with all the erotic day-dreams and the nightly fantasies in bed, where Elise had figured in more than a few of his overheated imaginings. He'd listened to the loose talk about her avidly, and not a little enviously. Men's talk. The general gist of which had remained unchanged for centuries. A boasting hotch-potch of wild exaggerations, half-truths and downright lies. Like Arthur Sullivan bragging that he'd made her four times in one evening. Behind the Jobbers' Arms.

'Do you believe that?'

'Not really . . . ' And it didn't matter. Not so long as she let him jump her, he thought, with the cheerful crudity of youth. He gave her an impudent smile. 'Perhaps I might feel that all your so-called 'experience' is to my advantage.'

'You might.' She leaned forward and put a hand on the tender male swell of him, the wicked glint in her eyes matching that in his own. 'You very well might, bucko.'

Seth knew he'd won.

He grinned in relief. His. To have, and to hold.

'I know the cottage isn't exactly Buck House, my sweet,' he said, 'but it can be smartened up — '

Elise lifted her head and stared at him. He really meant it. 'And if Amos decides to return?' she asked quietly.

'He won't.'

'How can you be sure?'

'Because I killed him,' replied Seth simply.

5

Elise sat up straight, her green-gold eyes wide with shock.

'You *killed* him!

Seth nodded. 'That's right. And whatever else in life I might be sorry for, it'll never be that.' His voice roughened. 'He was fond of beating the living daylights out of the pair of us whenever he'd had a jar or two. It was almost a ritual, and we'd come to expect it. There was certainly nothing we could do about it — '

No, thought Elise, remembering the bulging muscles and bull strength of his father, there wouldn't be. Amos could, quite easily, have made mincemeat of his son. Physically, both Seth and Kathie took after their wisp of a mother who had died when Seth was twelve.

The gritty voice went on: 'Then I came home one day and found him rutting on Kathie . . . You asked me why I didn't return to Langdon House after Christmas

— well, there's your reason.' He turned to show her his back, the criss-cross of recently-healed scars a puckered web in the sunlight. 'So much for standing up to Amos. The one time I tried it he damned near crippled me . . . But I swore he'd pay — '

So Seth had bided his time. Had waited, in stark truth, for — how long? . . . Elise reckoned swiftly — three clear months and more. A fact more seriously against him than any killing in white-hot rage.

She fanned a hand and ran gentle fingers along his spine.

'It doesn't pain you now?'

He shook his head. 'And he won't do it again, will he?' His mouth twisted. 'Spawn of the Devil he called me. Well, maybe he was right, after all; he was a vile old devil and he got what he'd bred.'

Elise's first reaction had been shock; her second was a profound desire to protect him.

'Have you told anyone else of this?'

'No.' His eyes met hers. 'Only you.' And Elise he would trust beyond hell and back. 'I don't think anyone will ever find his body. On the other hand — ' He gave a shrug. 'Fate plays foul tricks . . . '

She licked her lips.

'Where is he? Amos. Where have you put him?'

The bright eyes turned to her, their expression blank.

'Best you don't know,' he said.

'I have to, Seth. If I'm going to marry you, live here, tread these floors, maybe dig this garden . . . '

A crack of smile. 'He's nowhere around here. You'll not tumble over him by accident, that I promise you. But best let his resting-place remain my secret.'

For the moment she left it at that. Later, she might persuade him to tell her, if she thought it was necessary. Just now it didn't seem important.

'Kathie, does she know?'

He shrugged. 'She must suspect. But I didn't kill him in front of her, if that's what you mean.'

That wasn't what she had meant, but he had answered her question. Of course Kathie knew. The wild eyes and hunted manner told her Kathie knew. But Kathie loved her brother. No danger there.

Through the window she could see the girl wandering aimlessly around the garden. She was wearing a torn and shapeless garment in a faded shade of blue, and her long hair was uncombed and crowned in daisies, and fell in elf-locks about her face. She looked like some dirty, demented Ophelia.

Something would have to be done about Kathie.

'Let's all go to the watchtower,' said Elise suddenly, leaping out of bed. Anywhere. To shake free of this place.

Seth eyed her with amusement.

'Certainly. Like that?'

Elise grabbed her clothes. 'We'll take a picnic lunch to the tower hill and forget what has to be done around here for a while . . . ' She felt the need for sunshine and some good fresh air.

'Okay.' He watched her dress in silence, then slipped out of bed and stood up beside her, reaching across her to the dressing-table to pick up the heavy bracelet she had been wearing the night before. It was an old-fashioned, snake-linked affair from which swung large pieces of roughly shaped black stone on tarnished chains.

'Don't forget your rocks,' he growled, sliding the chain over her hand and pulling tight the locking device. He eyed the burnished stones curiously. 'What's it made of? Coal?'

'Jet, I think,' she replied, her eyes meeting his in the mirror with a smile. 'It was my grandmother's. It's of no great worth, except in curiosity value, but I'm fond of it.'

'Comes in useful as a cosh, no doubt.' He grinned, and reached for his trousers. 'Ready when you are.'

Kathie did not particularly want to spend her time picnicking at the watch-tower, nor anywhere else, for that matter, but, then, neither did she wish to be left behind, for unquestionably Seth would go there anyway, with Elise. And she guessed what that would mean! No longer was it the two of them, brother and sister, against the world. He had changed his allegiance.

Stinking whore!

Dejectedly, she trailed along behind them.

'*White, White, your head's not right, Turn it around, and screw it on tight.*'

The Burns brothers again, by the bridge. Up to their ankles in the river Chatton. They were catching minnows in a jar.

Kathie prayed that a bolt from heaven would strike them down; that a streak of lightning would flash from the sky and burn them up from the crowns of their sandy fair hair to the soles of their Wellington boots. Or that Seth would somehow put the evil-eye on them . . .

'Clear off home, lads,' said Seth amiably, too comfortable for once to wish ill on others. Life was good. His body throbbed with well-being.

'Do they do that often?' asked Elise, glancing behind her as she, Seth, and Kathie started up the steep incline towards the watchtower.

'Not so much now. It was Amos they preferred tormenting; he always rose to their bait.' He spoke as if Amos were already long gone into the past; as if he, Seth, had sloughed off everything he could of his father as quickly and painlessly as possible.

'Why didn't you leave him?' asked Elise suddenly, stretching out to take Seth's left hand in her right. 'Your father. Why didn't you and Kathie run off?'

'Where to?'

He flung himself down on the daisy-splattered grass and closed his eyes.

Lowering herself more gently beside him, Elise sat clasping her crooked-up knees. Extraordinary, this passionate tenderness that filled her for him. The sun beat down upon them, hot as it would become that day. And unseasonable for April. She ached to lean over and cover that tight-set face with kisses, to draw his lath-like body to her and hold it close. To make slow and sensual love to him. She did none of those things, but sat staring into the infinite distance. Time enough for that, my love, she promised him silently. Time enough for that shattering, inescapable, ecstatic loss of self.

She sat quite still on top of the visible

world, with the rich folds of the fields and woods rolling away beneath her, every shade of green and brown under the sun, with sudden brilliant splashes of ochre where the gorse bloomed against a sky of cloudless blue. Nearby, Kathie knelt stringing flowers stalk through stalk, more relaxed than Elise had so far seen her.

Maybe this outing had not been such a bad idea.

After they had eaten, Elise wandered across to the foot of the watchtower, but the way in was barred by a chain and padlock on the door.

'We can't get to the top,' she said in disappointment, coming back to Seth. 'It's locked.'

'We'll see about that,' retorted Seth, scrambling to his feet. She watched him cross to make his own investigations.

'There you are,' he called.

The door was standing wide.

'How did you *do* that?' Elise ran to his side.

'By fantastic skill,' chuckled Seth.

'By a hefty great clout, more like,' retorted Elise, examining the lock and hasp. 'You've broken it.'

He shrugged. 'You wanted to go up.'

No point in arguing further; the door was open. And she made her way cautiously up the twisting stairs. Here and there they had crumbled away and the bends had to be negotiated carefully. But the view when they reached the top was worth the effort. It was superb. Roofless and eroded, the edifice stood with its four look-out points braced to the four winds, giving an all-round panorama of the surrounding countryside.

'It's ages since I was up here,' said Elise, going to the far window-embrasure and looking down. The giddy height almost took her breath away. The watchtower was built on the edge of the cliff and, on that side, the drop was sheer to the murderous tumble of rocks below.

She leaned out. 'My grandmother was supposed to have flown from here.'

'Do you believe it?'

'No, of course not. Perhaps they were more gullible in those days. But I wish I'd known her.' She leaned further forward.

'It really feels as if one could. Fly, I mean. As if one could launch oneself into space and sail away, held up like a cork in water by all that polished air below.'

'I shouldn't try,' Seth remarked dryly. 'You'd come to earth with an awful wallop.' He hunched a shoulder against the wall and gave himself up to the shameless pleasure of watching her.

Throwing him a brief, abstracted smile, Elise stepped to her left and walked over to gaze through the eastern embrasure. The church tower and the top of the rectory chimneys were visible from there, although the rest of the village was hidden by trees.

Turning to Seth, she said abruptly: 'What do you think of the new rector?'

'I've not had much to do with him,' he replied cautiously.

'He's suggested that I might like to work for him — helping Mrs Pawcett a couple of times a week. Do the rough, that sort of thing.'

'And will you?'

'I don't know. I might. If I can fit it in with Langdons.' She rested her elbows on the sill and her chin in her hands. 'There are worse jobs.'

He quirked an eyebrow. 'Such as the Langdons?'

'No, not Langdons. I like it there.'

'Ill-starred place, that. Langdon House. Nothing but trouble and bad luck there for years. The sooner you jack it in, the better. They've a nasty reputation for losing staff. What with one leaping from this watchtower, and another getting her throat cut . . .'

'That was years and years ago. Besides, she didn't get her throat cut. She was tortured to make her reveal where the family diamond had been hidden. You know the story. *Adamant* scrawled in blood . . .'

While she had been speaking, Elise had taken herself back across the room and was now leaning through the south window-embrasure again, trying to see the white gleam of the fallen rocks far below her. Her dress had pulled tightly across her haunches, moulding the flesh beneath into delectable, peach-like curves, and the hem of the skirt had ridden up almost indecently to expose a tormenting expanse of long bare leg and satiny, parted thighs.

Seth felt a slow heat spreading through him, a pounding of his pulses, and knew he wanted to push her back against the wall and make love to her, then and there. Quick and finished. And might have done so, had Kathie not loomed suddenly in the doorway.

He smothered a curse beneath his breath.

'I'm going home,' Kathie said.

That was all right; they were all going home. Glittering-eyed, he followed his sister through the door, and preceded Elise down the winding stairs. With every step she took he was able to catch a provocative glimpse of her shapely legs above him. God, but when they got back to the cottage he was going to take her to bed and keep her there . . .

The brisk walk home was filled with the most intense and pleasurable anticipation.

Elise, however, had other ideas. On reaching their destination she refused to go in, saying she wanted first to cut across the fields to Langdons, to apologize for her morning's absence, and then to return to her own place for fresh clothes. Worse, the evening and night she intended to spend, not with him, but at the Goodes' farmhouse on the Downs.

'I promised Ruby Goode I'd stay there tonight,' said Elise. 'Her husband has to be away, and she can't face being alone. Understandable, I suppose. I'd like to hamstring that wretched driver.' She turned to Seth, aware that he had become very still. He was paper-white, and his eyes had taken on an unnatural, unseeing look, the pupils dilated under expressionless brows.

'Seth.' She stared at him anxiously; he looked ill, or was that sick look anger? He seemed to be controlling himself only with an effort. 'I'll be back in the morning. I must go to Mrs Goode's tonight. I promised. I can't let her down; she's expecting me. I can't leave her alone at a time like this, not with the death of her boy having occurred so recently. If there were any way of wriggling out of it,

I would. But I can't.'

The muscles of his face were stiff with his desire for her, but he managed to say in a gritty voice: 'No, of course not . . . See you tomorrow, then?' And he whirled and strode after his sister into the house.

6

Bevan Oake surveyed his breakfast through bilious eyes.

'Aye. It's cold,' said Mrs Pawcett, fixing him with a gimlet stare. 'You'd be cold if you'd been sitting half an hour uncovered on a plate.' She sniffed. 'Of course, if you'd had the sense to tell me what you were going to do, I could've kept it warm. But I'm not clairvoyant.'

'You let Elise in,' pointed out Bevan mildly. 'You knew she was here.'

'Here, yes. But naturally I assumed she would have had the grace to postpone her discussion until you'd eaten,' rejoined Mrs Pawcett with asperity.

'She'd to be at Langdon House for work by nine.'

Mrs Pawcett snorted. In her opinion, that young madam's work was done considerably later in the day.

The interview had not been an unqualified success, reflected Bevan, mourning the changes a few short days could bring, and blaming himself bitterly for the coming marriage of Elise to Seth White. If he'd not encouraged the girl to go to the Whites . . . But impossible, now, to undo the wrong. He had tried to persuade both Seth and Elise to think again. Marriage, after all, was not a step to be taken lightly. And Seth was very young. But they had been immovable: they knew what they were doing. Indeed, they had been living together for several days now, it was common gossip . . .

'Jim Burns came while you were closeted with madam,' went on Mrs Pawcett. 'He wouldn't wait. Said Arthur Sullivan's been after his Peggy again. Fourteen, she is.' She squeezed out a thin smile. 'Not that I don't say as she's not been giving the fellow the 'come on'.'

'I don't see what I can do,' said Bevan. 'It would be more to the point if her father had a quiet word with the pair of them. Explained the dangers.'

'Burns is far past the quiet-word stage,' said Mrs Pawcett testily. Her eyes locked on Bevan. 'Anyhow, I'm relaying the man's message. If Arthur Sullivan touches young Peggy again, he'll get his neck broken!'

Bevan sighed and stuck a fork into the congealed mess on his plate.

Jonathan, who had breakfasted on hot egg and bacon at the proper time, wheeled into the room.

'How goes the morning, Brother?' he inquired with a grin.

'Foul,' said Bevan.

'Ah, the impending nuptials of the fair Elise and young Seth White . . . The village whore and the local lout. Should prove interesting.' Jonathan gave his brother a beaming smile. 'That should teach you to keep your fingers out of village pies — '

'Cade Burrell seemed to think it was a good idea,' mumbled Bevan, through rubberised egg. 'He agreed with me that Elise would be a fit person to give Amos' children a friendly hand.'

Mrs Pawcett raised her eyebrows. 'I should have thought Cade Burrell was the last person with whom to discuss Elise Walters,' she remarked tartly.

'Why do you say that?' Bevan looked up.

'They were once engaged. Years ago. Cried off on the eve of the wedding.'

'Who cried off?'

'Some say one, and some say t'other. but I have my own ideas on that subject, and you can take it from me that Cade Burrell's not overfond of the ladies.'

'Well, he wouldn't be, would he, if he were jilted at the altar?' said Bevan reasonably.

'You mean he's queer, Mrs Pawcett?' Jonathan, having caught the nuance, flicked a bright glance up at her. 'Really? Cade Burrell?'

'There's queer and queer,' replied Mrs Pawcett. 'Just say that, if I had a teenage lad I'd not want him hanging around at Burrell's. And there was all that trouble with Michael Goode — the eldest Goode boy, that is — a few years back. Nearly lived in Burrell's pocket he did. Nobody knows for certain what happened — except his parents, and they're not telling — But next thing we know, young Michael's off to London, and we've seen neither hair nor hide of him since.'

'Youngsters do that every day,' protested Bevan. 'Pull up sticks and go off to the big city, I mean. There's nothing very sinister in that. People make me sick. If a fellow's not chasing girls all the time they think he must be odd. And not just odd, but bent!' He scowled.

Mrs Pawcett shrugged and applied a duster to the mantelpiece.

'I'd say Elise Walters would be the best judge of that,' she said, 'seeing as how she was brought up in the Burrell household. Mrs Burrell — Cade's mother — took the child in after her parents died. Hand in glove, Cade and Elise. Always were.' She flicked the duster across Jonathan's wheelchair. 'Until she tried to get him to the altar — '

'Mrs Pawcett,' said Bevan in irritation, 'I do wish you wouldn't dust the dining-room while we are still eating breakfast. It's most unhygienic.'

'You're supposed to have finished breakfast,' said his housekeeper haughtily. 'Ages ago. And I've too much to do to hang around here any longer. Run off my feet, I am. I don't think you young gentlemen appreciate — '

She launched into a familiar tale of woe.

Bevan poured another cup of coffee and said sweetly: 'I do understand, Mrs Pawcett, believe me. This place is much too large for you to manage on your own. However — ' He threw her a rallying smile ' — I have ventured to persuade Elise Walters to come in for a couple of days a week, to give you a helping hand.'

Mrs Pawcett scowled. 'I don't want any helping hand,' she said. 'Leastways, not from the likes of her.'

'That wasn't what you were saying a few moments ago,' protested Bevan. 'You were moaning that the house was too much for you.'

'Not moaning,' said Mrs Pawcett, 'just airing my views. And I don't want Elise cluttering up the place. *Elise*. Now there's high-falutin' for you. Her mother did be calling her Elsie, I'm thinking.'

'She's a good worker, by all accounts.'

'She is that. She'd work on you fast enough, at any rate.'

'I am about to join her and Seth White in holy matrimony,' said Bevan with clerical pomposity.

Jonathan threw him a speculative look. 'Removing temptation, Brother?' he asked softly.

Bevan rose from the table and collected a pile of books from the sideboard. The discussion, as far as he was concerned, was at an end.

Mrs Pawcett was still glaring at him.

'Elise Walters wouldn't have a clue how this rectory is run.'

'Then you find her a clue, like a good Mrs Pawcett,' said Bevan, patting her shoulder as he passed. 'I'm sure you won't regret it.'

'But you might,' said Mrs Pawcett darkly. 'I'm giving you a word of advice, Rector — '

'Is it likely to be a long word?' asked Bevan, 'because I'm busy.'

'I'm telling you, steer clear of Elise Walters. There's enough queer goings on in this village without you opening your doors to a witch.'

Bevan stared at her, open-mouthed.

'Like grandmother, like great-grand-mother — ' enlarged Mrs Pawcett. 'How else do you account for her going through nearly all the men in Chatton Eastwood?'

'Sex appeal.'

'She bewitched them,' insisted Mrs Pawcett.

'What utter and absolute rubbish.' Bevan's eyes were like grey stones.

'Oh, you can call it rubbish if you choose, but I'm telling you . . . If she sets her mind on a man, then he'd be a fool to cross her — '

'A blind fool,' agreed Jonathan with a smile. 'She's very pretty.' Again that speculative glance towards his brother.

'Cade Burrell made quite a success of it, though, from what you've been telling me,' said Bevan nastily.

'That,' said Mrs Pawcett with lofty disdain, 'was different.' She returned to her theme. 'All that family have had peculiar powers. Ask anyone — '

'Well, she's not likely to run off with the spoons,' snapped Bevan.

'She's a great-granddaughter of Mercy Goodbright,' said Mrs Pawcett, as if that clinched the matter.

Mercy Goodbright had been a nineteenth-century witch; that much Bevan had recently found out for himself. She had been a purely local phenomenon and her activities had been confined to the one or two villages around Chatton Eastwood. But, whatever tricks she had pulled, Bevan was far from convinced that her gifts were supernatural. In his opinion, she had been an arch con-woman and had undoubtedly thoroughly enjoyed herself.

That there was documented evidence of her so-called powers came about solely because her death had taken place in the local market town, in the present town hall. In earlier times she would unquestionably have hanged, but by the late eighteen-hundreds there was no punishment for witchcraft and none meted out for such, except that which might be taken on hand by a frightened populace.

'That was a very long time ago,' said Bevan. Yet that was the one sure thing about a village; it never let you forget. And feuds and rivalries could sometimes last through centuries.

'Others had — and have — that same power,' said Mrs Pawcett darkly. 'It got handed down, here and there. The Power . . . Power to call up the Devil, to walk through walls. To fly — '

'That's utter nonsense.'

'That kind of thing never dies. Not completely. Sometimes it becomes watered down a little, goes underground for a while. Even gets turned into something less malevolent — '

'Sublimated,' said Jonathan.

'I expect you're right,' agreed Mrs Pawcett hazily. 'Anyhow, it gets handed on, in one form or another.'

'The seventh-child-of-a seventh-child syndrome,' murmured Jonathan, adding with cold irony: 'Not many of those around these days, I should imagine.'

'There's no such thing as witchcraft,' said Bevan firmly. 'Then, or now. And I can't think of any good reason why Elise shouldn't work here.'

'I can think of plenty of not good reasons,' snarled Mrs Pawcett. 'All the Goodbrights have been peculiar. The name's gone now, but the blood still runs in a lot of the veins around here. Causes a great deal of unrest from time to time, I can tell you. Like that business with Marnie Bunch — same blood, see — and the Reverend Honeysett.' She frowned. 'Mercy Goodbright had twin daughters. One of them was Elise Walters' grandmother, and you know what happened to *her*.'

'No, I don't,' said Bevan flatly. 'Enlighten me.'

'She flew from the watchtower, cool as you please. Flew away and was never seen again.'

'Oh, *really*, Mrs Pawcett.' Bevan stared at his housekeeper in disgust. 'You can't truly believe that. Not in this day and age.'

'She flew,' said Mrs Pawcett obstinately. 'From the top of the old watchtower.'

'That's just superstitious nonsense. The wretched woman must have jumped.'

'Then how come no one ever found her body?' demanded Mrs Pawcett with her own irrefutable logic. 'They searched below, but not a trace of her could they find. She had gone. Taken off into thin air, and away.'

'With or without her broomstick?' grinned Jonathan.

Bevan scowled at him, then returned to Mrs Pawcett.

'Rubbish. Her body must have been caught up somewhere, maybe in a crevice, or among bushes. There are fallen rocks there . . . '

'Everywhere was examined thoroughly. Over and over again. It would be, wouldn't it? To scotch the rumours. And to satisfy people like you.' Mrs Pawcett looked at him smugly. 'No. She flew like a bird.'

'What a singular thing to wish to do,' said Jonathan, his eyes dancing.

'Mock all you please,' responded Mrs Pawcett with dignity, 'but facts are facts. She was seen. By at least a dozen people. And the then rector among them. You're not doubting the word of the cloth, are you?' She scowled at Bevan. 'My own mother was an eyewitness. Up in the church tower, they were. At the dedication of the new flagpole. A whole party of them. The watchtower can be seen from there, plain as a pikestaff. And that's not all. A couple of tramps near the lower bridge saw her, too. Saw her launch into the air and sail away. Only they were too afraid to come forward immediately. They had evidently been poaching on Frognalls estate, and had the spoils on them. So they took to their heels and ran like the clappers.'

'And is that the only thing she ever did, then, to substantiate her claim to being a witch?' asked Bevan dryly.

'Indeed it was not. She could fly. She could walk through walls. She could ill wish and make it stick — Everyone was afraid of her. You ask the Langdons. It was she who put the curse on the Langdon diamond. '*No safe will be able to hold it*',' she quoted glibly. 'Nor could one.'

'I can't imagine anyone in their right senses believing a word of it.' Bevan's mouth curved mockingly. 'But I suppose the stone conveniently disappeared.'

'Yes, it did.'

'Up the witches,' grinned Jonathan.

'Well, the lady of Langdon House evidently believed it,' said Mrs Pawcett with spirit, 'and she was leaving nothing to chance, because while her husband was away on business she devised some other hiding-place for the gem. With the help of her faithful abigail. When Langdon returned he found the place ransacked, the staff locked in the cellar, his wife and her maid-servant dead, and one word scrawled in the young girl's blood. *Adamant*.' Mrs Pawcett was enjoying herself hugely. 'The would-be thieves had tortured the girl to force her to reveal the secret, but it died with her. The diamond was never found.'

'Odd sort of thing for a servant-girl to write,' remarked Jonathan. 'And a bit pointless, wouldn't you say, to do it with her dying breath? Telling her master that she'd held out adamantly? Hell, he would be able to fathom that out for himself, wouldn't he? She'd died protecting her secret.'

'There's a theory that the girl could have been referring to the diamond itself. Adamant — merely another way of saying 'diamond' . . . That, after her torturers had left her and she realized she was dying, she'd tried to leave a message for her master, to tell him where the stone was hidden — but her strength gave out.'

'Poor little blighter. Fat lot of good her loyalty did her, or them. The stone was never found, you say. Probably the thieves waltzed off with it anyhow.'

'They said they didn't. They were caught soon afterwards and promised all kind of deals if they'd produce it . . . If they had it, they died for it.'

'And I dare say, from then on, Elise's grandmother's reputation as a witch went from strength to strength — ' Bevan's tone dripped sarcasm.

Mrs Pawcett regarded him doubtfully.

'Well, she flew from the tower next day — ' she said.

Bevan gripped his head in exasperation. 'Mrs Pawcett!'

'Sounds very foxy to me,' put in Jonathan, 'her going off like that so soon after the tragedy. Maybe she was the one who purloined the diamond . . . '

'How could she? She didn't know

where it had been hidden. No one did. The mistress told her husband she'd keep it secure, and not in the safe. He trusted her. She was a very astute woman, by all accounts ... Elise's grandmother was nowhere near Langdon House at the time. And never returned there.' Mrs Pawcett scowled at them. 'How could she? Cursing hens and pigs and diamonds is one thing; bringing about the death of an innocent serving-girl — a village girl — is quite another. They'd have done to her what they did to her mother, Mercy Goodbright. So she flew.'

'What did they do to her mother?' asked Jonathan.

'Oh, there's a plaque to her on the wall of the local town hall,' said Bevan dryly. 'You should see it some time.'

'To a witch?'

'Commemorating her death. Seems someone stuck a stake through her. One market-day.'

'That's for vampires.'

'Works well enough with witches, too, I should imagine,' said Bevan, even more dryly.

Mrs Pawcett regarded her duster thoughtfully.

'That kind of power doesn't forsake families like that. It pops up again and again. And around Chatton Eastwood there's been plenty of interbreeding over the years, with and without benefit of clergy.' A nodular finger prodded in Bevan's direction. 'I've told my granddaughter, Sally, to be sure and marry a stranger; that way she'll be certain not to get any tainted blood.'

'Mrs Pawcett. I don't believe this; I don't believe I'm having this conversation with you . . . '

'Unto the third and fourth generation,' said Mrs Pawcett firmly.

'Should be wearing thin by now, then,' said Jonathan, laughter bubbling in his voice.

Mrs Pawcett twisted on him with a flash of eyes. 'Power like that never dies out, you remember that. The Reverend Honeysett saw fit to take a swing at it — and crazed as a coot he was, when carried out from here. And little Marnie, in her grave. Oh, not wise to

meddle, Mr Jonathan; not wise at all
. . . Especially now something's abroad
again.'

'What do you mean?'

'Night meetings in the churchyard.
And black candles burning. Chickens
beheaded, and their entrails strewn on
doorsteps — '

'I've not heard anything of it,'
protested Bevan. 'No one's said anything
to me.'

'Well, they wouldn't, would they?
You're not one of us. But, take it from
me, there's been plenty of such nasty
goings on; has been for months. The
writing's been on the wall . . . ' She
obviously meant it quite literally.

'Are you talking about cabalistic signs?'
demanded Jonathan. 'Pentagons and
magic circles and the like?'

Mrs Pawcett nodded. 'And things
disappear. Or are taken for some beastly
ritual, or other.' She swung to Bevan
again. 'If you cast your mind back, you'll
recall that the church itself was entered,
a while ago; candles, stolen . . . and
Communion wine — '

'A classic case of pilfering,' retorted Bevan. 'An ever-present hazard of the unlocked building.'

'Bolts and bars are no deterrent. Mrs Lee lost several hens. Locked in the hen-house they were, and next morning — gone.'

'A fox,' said Bevan.

'Must have had pretty big teeth, then,' said Mrs Pawcett with spirit. 'The lock was snapped.'

'So. Petty theft. Simple enough to do; a lever on a crowbar, a bang with a hammer . . .'

'And that makes noise. Bess didn't wake.'

'Maybe she sleeps soundly.'

'Bess is the guard dog, and she's trained to wake. Besides, there was more — A three-tined fork there, used for hay; all twisted out of shape, it was. Like an obscene mockery of a cross. And thrust, point down, into the earth — '

'Difficult for it to have been thrust into the earth in any other way, I should have thought,' said Bevan crushingly. 'Mrs Pawcett, we don't wish to stir up all that muddy water again. It's finished. *Finished!*'

'Is it?' said Mrs Pawcett. She looked at him fondly, as one might look at an idiot child. 'Well then, dear, we shall see — '

7

Bevan sighed. One imagined such beliefs were dead, then there they were again, raising their evil heads. He knew how it was: he'd grown up in a small, isolated village himself. That, too, had had its resident witch. A harmless enough soul, when it came down to it, but treated with care. Ah, yes. Treated with extreme care. But black magic, now, that was something different, a more organised — and recurring — type of menace. It seemed that there was always someone ready to fan those embers . . .

He afforded his housekeeper a frown. 'I'd be grateful, Mrs Pawcett, if you would assist me in scotching these witchcraft rumours — '

'You can't stop people talking,' she said. 'We have a history in Chatton Eastwood of the darker side of nature.'

'Poppycock!'

'That's not very nice, that's not.'

'Mrs Pawcett,' said Bevan wearily. 'I've a funeral to see to; I'm not feeling particularly nice.'

'Ah, yes. Young Robin. Well, that's what I mean, see,' said an unrepentant Mrs Pawcett. 'Queer goings on . . . Now you can't call that child's death a natural event — '

'I suppose a hit-and-run tragedy might not be exactly construed as — '

'That wasn't what I meant,' said Mrs Pawcett crossly. 'If you'd take the trouble to ask around, to listen, you'd know what folks are saying. It wasn't natural. Not natural at all. What was the boy doing on the Hatchins road, tell me that?'

'Children roam all over. Places they're not supposed to go, half the time.'

'He was on his way to his friends. To the Burns brothers. And they live over on Fairfield, the other side of Frognalls bridge.'

'Well, maybe he decided to try a different route, or to potter off to see someone else first. Or maybe he was taking a short cut, or something. Oh, I don't know. There could have been any number of reasons why he was there.'

'Have you ever tried taking a short cut to Frognalls via the Hatchins road?' asked Mrs Pawcett contemptuously.

'No. But — '

'Our Sally saw him. He passed her that day on the lower road, and that's clear all the way down to Frognalls bridge. No turn-offs, no nothing.'

'Maybe he back-tracked.'

'Sally'd have seen him.'

'Well, maybe Sally had her eyes shut. If it disturbs anyone, why wasn't it mentioned to the police?'

'The police,' spat out Mrs Pawcett in scorn. 'What would they do? Ask a damn lot of silly questions, that's what. And keep honest folk from their work. Then they'd like as not point a finger in the wrong direction. Doesn't pay to say too much to the police, it doesn't. They didn't do much about poor Lisha White, when her husband fair near beat her to death. Domestic affair, they called it. Domestic affair, my arm!' She scowled. 'Besides, they couldn't bring young Robin back, could they?'

No, thought Bevan, nothing could do that. And it had seemed a pretty clear cut and dried case. Something had hit the child's bicycle and spun it into a ditch. The boy had broken his neck against a section of stone wall there ... He frowned momentarily. But it did seem an odd way round to Frognalls.

Sally Pawcett. Now there was a wasp-tongued female, if you like! Keen, though, he'd give her that. Fifteen years old and as sharp as a needle. If the uncharming Miss Pawcett said she saw Robin on his way along the road to Frognalls, then he, Bevan, would personally have placed a bet that Robin had been on his way along it.

But that wasn't possible. Unless he'd flown!

'What do you make of that, then?' asked Bevan, when Mrs Pawcett had left the room.

Jonathan laughed. 'The biggest load of eyewash since Aladdin rubbed his lamp. And yet ... ' He frowned over towards the window. 'They're not all turnip heads, are they? They read, watch television, travel out and about. They've been to school — And Mrs Pawcett, on one of her better days, is a bright enough little body, with a whole mint of common sense — '

'Not showing much of it today, then, is she? Behaving like a right banana.' Bevan stared at his brother. 'You didn't *believe* her; not about Elise's grandmother and all that cursing and flying nonsense? Jonathan! There's no such thing as witchcraft; no such thing as invoking the devil, or ability to cast spells. It's all in people's minds. If someone believes in a curse then, possibly, the darn thing will happen, but not because of any voodoo or intervention by Old Nick.'

'I know that,' said Jonathan shortly.

'So, some old biddy, years ago, utters a curse and, coincidentally, something dire duly happens. Her reputation is enhanced. The next time she seems likely to become a bit put out about something, people are going to hurry to placate her, aren't they? Human nature. They don't really believe in all that nonsense, but best to play safe — Oh, yes.'

'So you think it was coincidence that

the diamond disappeared, a girl was murdered and another jumped — or flew! — from the watchtower?'

'Of course. Don't you?'

'In the bright light of day, yes. But when one is alone, and the wind howls in the chimneys and the house creaks in the storm; when darkness falls, and the electric light fails; when one's very bones turn to water ... ah, what then, Brother — ?' Jonathan grinned across at him.

'Don't be so ridiculous.'

'And suppose you believed in your own powers? Suppose you believed you really were a witch — ? Suppose Elise's grandmother really believed she could do the things she said she could, what then? ... She had evidently been gunning for the Langdons — probably one of them had crossed her up at some time — but I doubt if she'd meant to harm that girl — '

'No,' said Bevan slowly., 'I don't suppose she did.' He raised his head thoughtfully. 'You mean she might very well have jumped from that watchtower, in remorse? . . . Possible, I suppose. But that still doesn't explain her missing body — ' He frowned. 'It's Elise I feel sorry for. Growing up with all that welter of superstition at her back. And doubtlessly aware that if anything odd happens in her vicinity it'll be attributed to her. Even the fact that she's pretty and patently sexy is seen, not as something fairly normal, but as a form of power.'

'It doesn't appear to have hurt her.' Jonathan shot his brother an upward glance. 'Since she's been with Seth, she's blossomed like the rose.'

'Yes, I suppose so. I hope they'll be happy.'

'Do you? I'd say you're kicking yourself, Brother. But then, you always were rather slow off the mark and inclined to an inflated sense of your own importance.'

'Don't be more stupid than you can help, Jonathan.'

Jonathan shot his brother a bright-eyed, malicious smile and wheeled himself over to the window, where, for a moment, he stared out along the deserted drive.

'God, but we need someone to liven up this tomb.'

* * *

Elise had left the rectory in a buoyant frame of mind. She was going to marry Seth and no one was going to stop her; not Amos, not the villagers, not even the tricksy parson himself, who had so blatantly encouraged her to go to the Whites' cottage in the first place . . .

She smiled. They had received their first wedding present that morning, from Cade Burrell; an antique, chased silver teapot-stand, shaped in the form of a tripod. Seth had been childishly pleased with the gift.

When this you see, remember me, thought Elise, wryly, as she swung on her way.

The day was sunny and her steps were light, and, as yet, it was early; too early to contemplate with any joy incarcerating herself away from the sun in Langdon House. Halting, she sat on the warm, grassy bank beside the road, enjoying the beauty of the morning and idly scrawling with a stick in the dust at her feet.

Elise and Seth. Elise loves Seth. Seth loves Elise.

A boot swung suddenly across to obliterate her work.

Elise's head shot up.

Arthur Sullivan was standing there, grinning down at her. Her heart gave a little skip of dismay.

'Very distant lately, aren't we?' he said. 'How about tonight?'

'Not tonight, or any other night, Arthur,' said Elise, rising to her feet and brushing down her skirt.

'Oh, so that's the way the land lies, is it?'

'I'm afraid so. Those times have ended.'

'Not by a long chalk they haven't.' His tone was uncomfortably threatening.

Elise kept her good humour with difficulty.

'I must go, Arthur. I have to be at work by nine.'

'Should have considered that sooner, shouldn't you? Been hanging about the rectory long enough.'

'Spying, then, were we?' asked Elise sweetly. She flung him an exasperated look. 'If you must know — and you'll hear of it soon enough, anyway — I'm going to help out at the rectory.'

He grabbed her arm. 'What's Reverend Oake's interest in you, then? The same as most men's?'

'Wash your mouth out, Arthur Sullivan. And stop being so infantile . . . And let go of my arm, you're hurting me.'

He released his grip and she took a step away from him.

'So you'll not be down at the Jobbers' Arms tonight?' he growled.

'No. I'll be at the cottage with Seth.'

Arthur glared at her. 'Good God, Elise. You can't be serious about Seth White. He's only a pawky kid. You're taking in a boy to do a man's job, girl — '

Elise began walking away, but he fell into step behind her.

'What do you see in him, tell me that? It's hardly his fantastic body, is it? — little runt — unless he tucks all his muscles in one place!' He grabbed her arm again, forcing her to halt and swinging her round. 'But he'll not keep you satisfied for long, girl, you mark my words. You'll come crawling back to your usual haunts soon enough.'

'Let go of me,' said Elise, from between her teeth.

'When I'm good and ready.'

'Let go of me or — '

'Or what?' He pushed his face close to hers. 'I should humour me, if I were you, Elise Walters. Talk and act real pretty . . . ' He grinned. 'Because if you don't — '

'If I don't?' Her voice was dangerous.

'Then I might just upset your apple cart.'

She gazed at him with stormy eyes. 'You wormy creep . . . What the hell do you think you can do?'

Her anger served only to excite him. He took hold of both her upper arms and pulled her against him, kissing her roughly and wetly on the mouth. When she struggled it merely added more fuel to his flames, and with one hard cuff he knocked her down and flung himself heavily across her. Elise gave a strangled gasp as the breath was rammed out of her, then began fighting in earnest. The weight of his body pinned her down and she found it impossible to bring up her knee to strike him where she knew it would cause most damage. He was immensely strong, able to contain her with little effort, and already his fingers were on her skirts, dragging them upwards towards her waist. Twisting her hands in his hair she yanked back his head.

Arthur gave a grunt of pain, but immediately forced his mouth down again to hers, then as suddenly collapsed and rolled away to one side, clutching at his skull.

Panting, released, Elise stared up.

Seth was standing just above her, holding a short stave in his hand.

'Just a gentle tap,' he grinned, 'to teach him manners.' He bent towards her, and offered her his hand.

Pleasantly aromatic, the smell from crushed leaves of ploughman's spikenard drifted all about them as she scrambled into a sitting position.

Before she had time to do more than take a deep breath, the older man's fist was again moving purposefully in their direction.

'Seth! Look out,' she cried.

Seth spun.

'Naughty,' he chid, and wielded his stave once more with arrant enthusiasm.

Arthur went face to the ground and stayed there.

'Are you all right, love?'

Elise nodded. 'I told you how it would be — '

'And I told you it didn't matter.' He put an arm around her and helped her to her feet, and grinned again, hefting his stave. 'Sooner or later everyone's going to get the message.'

'I'm going to kill you,' spluttered Arthur, spitting soil. 'I'm going to kill you, bloody Seth White.' He lurched groggily to his knees.

Seth, even with a weapon, would be no match for a rabid Arthur Sullivan, face to face and ready. Elise hurriedly turned away and furnished herself with half a fencing stake.

'I'm going to — ' Arthur was on his feet, swaying, his eyes bloodshot with pain and fury. 'I'll fix you good and proper.' For a moment, madness stared from his eyes.

'Cut along, Arthur,' said Seth amiably. 'We don't want to make a meal of it.' He grinned. 'No hard feelings. The best man won.'

His opponent took a lunging step towards him, saw Elise with her back-up weapon poised and considered discretion the better part of valour. He swung and headed off in the opposite direction.

'I'll put a spoke in your wheel,' he shouted savagely over his shoulder. 'See if I don't.'

'Any time,' called back Seth cheerily.

Elise was truly frightened now. She had seen and heard the venom in the older man and had grown up with the stories of those who had taken on Arthur Sullivan — and lost. Dislocated arms, cracked ribs, broken teeth and shattered noses; it was not a pretty saga.

So far he had stopped short of killing. But barely short.

'Don't cross him, Seth,' she pleaded. 'Keep well out of his way; he can be nasty.'

'So can I,' said Seth mildly. 'So can I.'

8

Sunny April roared into sodden May, and May into June as the sun came out again. The wide-eyed dandelions along the roadside verges turned into ephemeral 'clocks' and sailed away on every puff of wind across hedges rusted over with dying hawthorn blossom. And the elder-trees foamed into curdled, creamy bloom.

With midsummer fast approaching, Seth and Elise had already been man and wife for several weeks on the morning that the Burns brothers started out to cycle to Chatton quarry.

Everywhere was lush and green and flower-scented as the three boys pumped their slow way up the long, tough incline towards the disused chalk quarry on the outskirts of the village. A favourite play area for the young fry in summer, it none the less took a great deal of muscle-power to get there, and a fine day to make it worthwhile. Days of curtaining rain sealed the place off as effectively as a ten-foot wall.

Now, sweating, winded, the youngest lad was flagging badly, and exhaustion quivered in every length of his erratic progression along the pitted tarmac.

Seeing his predicament, the other two boys put their feet to the ground and waited with ill-concealed impatience for him to catch up.

'Told you to stay home,' growled Cliff, the eldest, in an unfeeling tone.

'Keep going,' wheezed Sam valiantly, poppy-faced and panting. 'I'm doing my best. It's this rotten bike. It's too small . . . ' He scowled at his front wheel and wobbled a wild curve across to them.

'You'll have us all piled up in the road, if you don't look out,' howled Cliff. 'Watch what you're doing!'

'If I could have a bike like yours — '

'You've been told, at Christmas.'

'That's years away.' Young Sam swerved towards the banking and remained there, his chest heaving.

The other two regarded him dispassionately.

'Why couldn't you have stayed at home?' sighed Cliff.

'Because!' puffed Sam. 'You and Adam have all the fun.' He plucked a blade of grass and squeaked it between his fingers and, for long seconds, no one added anything further to the conversation. 'There's Robin's bike,' he said at last, recovering some breath. 'D'you think I've a chance of that?'

'No chance.'

'But — '

'It was twisted out of shape. Useless. Fit only for scrap.'

'Cade Burrell says it could be straightened,' said Sam doggedly.

Cliff frowned. 'You're to keep away from him. Dad says he's a hommy, and . . . Aw, c'mon. The others'll be waiting for us at the quarry.' And he headed off, followed by Adam, his second-in-command.

With a frustrated sigh, Sam hauled himself upon his own despised means of transport once more, and prepared to pedal in the wake of his speedier brothers.

After the death of Robin Goode, Cliff

Burns had become unelected leader of the little gang. Lacking Robin's gifts of enterprise and invention, he was inclined to stick to the tried and tested order of things; tree-climbing, stone-throwing, wrestling, football — Nothing that demanded too much challenge. And his band was growing restless.

He watched them, now, from his vantage-point on a pile of rocks, a brawny, freckle-faced lad without grace of body, whose forehead already bore lines of anxiety stamped prematurely upon it. They were all there: his brother, Adam, one year younger than himself, and the most loyal and trusted member of the group, who was gathering the wherewithal to start a fire; the Pawcett boys, Joe and Teddy, ten-year-old twins (grandsons of Mrs Pawcett and brothers of Sally) both now trampling down the purple foxglove spires in abortive attempts to scale the chalk-face, along with Nevil Goode, a cousin of the dead Robin . . . And young Sam, at eight, the youngest.

Cliff's eyes flicked across to his brother,

Sam. He had told the child to sit and rest, and had left him to make his way across to the old car — an ancient Ford which had at sometime been stripped and tipped into the quarry. Devoid of everything that anyone could steal, its shell had become, in its time, all things to all people, from a shelter for the occasional tramp, to a target for the budding sharpshooter, and regularly transformed by the local children into whatever imagination happened to call for.

Sam was hunched across the bonnet of the derelict, green as a canful of mushy peas, being convulsively and noisily sick.

Hell! Leaping from his rock, Cliff raced across to him, his show of compassion induced more by the fear of what his mother would say if she found out that her youngling had been sorely overtaxed, than by any sense of sibling devotion.

'Steady, Sam. Steady. It's okay. I'm here.' Cliff held his youngest brother by the shoulders as the child heaved in distress across the car's bonnet. 'What's up? Did you get too hot, then?' Sam's eyes rolled back at him whitely. Sunstroke? Could it be sunstroke? Hell, he hoped not: his mother'd kill him for neglect . . .

'Okay, now, Sam?' He mopped the boy's face with his handkerchief. The greenish tinge seemed to be receding from the vomit-spattered flesh; from being pea-green, it was now merely pallid. Alternately mopping and exhorting his brother to 'bear up', Cliff staggered them both across to the stack of bicycles, where he was able to find a water-carrier and pour the younger boy a drink of water.

Sam promptly burst into tears.

'It's all right, young 'un. You'll feel better in a minute. Drink up,' said Cliff gruffly. 'Then we'll wash your face.' Glancing round first to make sure no one was looking, he put a clumsy, comforting arm around his brother.

Sam snuffled and hiccuped, and waved vaguely with one hand in the direction of the battered vehicle from which he had just been brotherly manhandled.

'In there,' he husked. 'He's in there. In the old car . . . Go look.' With a glurp, he turned about and started to retch again.

For a second or so, Cliff hovered over him, then wheeled and made his way back at a slow trot towards the car. It looked harmless enough. Reaching the front, he glanced through the doorless aperture to the driver's seat, where the padding oozed palely from the torn plastic. Nothing there. Only the stomach-churning smell of fresh vomit. And something else. A nauseating sweetness. Some kind of . . . booze, was it? Whisky? A bottle lay heeled on the floor, its contents long since gone. Leaning over the back of the seat he stared down into the rear compartment.

The next moment he had recoiled and, reeling blindly out into the sunshine, he, too, doubled over and was violently sick.

★   ★   ★

'Amos? They believe they've found Amos?' whispered Elise, whitening, and staring at Seth from frightened eyes. 'How? Where? . . . Is that possible?'

Seth raised his shoulders in a shrug.

120

His face, too, was white as chalk.

'Possible, obviously — although I'd not have thought it.' A small nerve twitched beside his left eye as he tried to smile at her. 'As to how and where . . . by children, in an abandoned car in the quarry.'

'In the *quarry*? You put his body in a car in the quarry?' cried Elise, incredulously.

'No. I said he was found there, that's all.'

'Then who put him there, if . . . ' She grabbed his arm. 'You buried him, didn't you? Seth. Where?'

'It doesn't seem to matter now, does it? One way or the other?' He unwrapped her fingers gently from his arm. 'I have to go. They want me to identify the body. That's what I came to tell you — '

'I'm coming with you.'

'No, love, I don't think that's wise.' He wished desperately that she would leave him alone. He was holding himself together only with an effort, and he was not sure how long he could continue to do so. The last thing he wanted was for his courage to crumble before her eyes. 'You must take care . . . ' he said. He patted her stomach, ran his hand upwards to her breast and cupped it there, feeling the heavy thud of her heart through his palm.

'I said I'm coming with you,' replied Elise firmly, pressing against him. If he went, he might not be coming back. Her heart skipped a terrified beat, but she kept her tone purposefully light. 'At the moment, Junior's little more than your wishful thinking, bucko, and what I see won't hurt him. Besides — ' she summoned up a grin ' — maybe the corpse isn't Amos. Whatever gives everybody the idea that it is?'

'Height and weight and general description, I suppose. And the fact they know he's missing.' His hands dropped slowly to his sides. 'I couldn't exactly admit that I thought otherwise.' He gave a brief smile. 'But you could be right. Maybe I'm panicking for nothing.'

'Seth. If it really is your father — ' She licked her lips. 'If by some means his body *has* landed up in the quarry . . . Is there any chance that his death might be taken to be an . . . accident?'

'I shouldn't think so,' he replied dryly. 'Let's face it, I knifed him. Several times.' He heard her breath draw in sharply, and said: 'It was the only way.' No point in going on about it. And what was done, was done.

After a minute, Elise said in a strained voice:

'But nobody can prove that *you* did it.'

She held to that fact all the way to the mortuary. No one could prove that Seth had killed his father. No one . . . Could they?

Beside her, Seth sat like death, staring straight ahead with wide, blind eyes, his hands clasped so hard in hers that the skin was blanched, and yet unresponsive to any pressure from her fingers, and as cold as stone.

And down the white corridors, too, unblinking still.

It would soon be over, Seth told himself. One way or another, it would soon be over. All he had to do was put one foot in front of the other . . . one foot in front of the other, until . . . And, if it were not Amos? If this were, indeed, some false alarm — ? His breathing became even more ragged. Was this how it was going to be? Always, from now on, every time someone discovered some unidentified body?

In a room over-lit and stark and as chilly as the corridors, he stared down at last at his putative and refrigerated dead. Stared for what seemed an eon, trying to regulate his breath, while the lights blinked and swung and pressed down upon him, flickering and fading from darkening walls. Until the floor rushed up to meet him.

From her position by the door, Elise saw him buckle and fall.

★　★　★

'Takes some of them like that,' said the attendant, handing Elise a cup of tea. 'Relief, see. They screw themselves up to some overstrung pitch, expecting to see God only knows what, and *twang*, they go down like released elastic when they've finished.'

'I don't like the look of him,' said Elise, her teeth chattering. Seth's skin was grey and his eyes were still shut. Stretched, unmoving, on a narrow bed in a small anteroom beyond the mortuary, he bore an unhealthy resemblance to a corpse himself. Only the slight rise and fall of his chest showed her that he lived. She must get him home, away from this place. Away from — Amos? The question was still there.

'He'll be all right in a minute,' said the attendant, 'they always are. But perhaps you'd like to take him home as soon as he comes round, come back again tomorrow?'

'Come back?' queried Elise faintly.

'Particulars,' said the attendant blithely. 'Forms, see. And the gentleman hasn't completed identification of the body. He keeled over, see. Not to worry, though.' He grinned cheerily. 'Tag number eight-stroke-four's not about to cut and run, is he?'

Elise gave a wan smile. 'I suppose not.' She cast a glance towards the bed. Seth's eyes were open now, large and black and shocked and, she thought, still unseeing.

'Was the old man a relative of yours?'

'My father-in-law,' said Elise. She turned, doubtfully. 'I knew him well. I could identify him myself, if that's allowed. It would save my husband — ' She glanced again at the bed.

'Sure. If you don't mind. Then, if it is your father-in-law, we can release the body to you for burial. Get everything tidied up neatly, like.'

'But I thought — ' Elise spun on him. 'The police — ?' She gestured towards the maze of corridors.

'The police'd have no further interest. Natural causes. The old boy died of a heart attack. Been drinking, of course. But, yes, heart attack. Nice and simple . . . '

★　★　★

'Why did you do it?' Sitting up in his own bed in the cottage, pale but recovering, Seth stared fixedly at his wife. His face looked gaunt and anxious and very young.

Elise made no sign of having heard his question.

'I think we'll have a fine day, tomorrow; the gnats were busy,' she said, picking up a hairbrush and applying it with vigour to her heavy mass of hair. The strands crackled with life at her touch and, under the light, it seemed that star-tipped trails of red caught fire and burned among the thick, rich darkness.

Seth's gaze remained sombre on her face.

'Elise, why'd you identify that dead man as Amos? You knew it wasn't. You must have known it wasn't. There was a superficial resemblance, I suppose, but you must've been aware that it was some nameless vagrant.'

'And therefore not likely to be missed,' said Elise calmly, continuing to brush her hair. 'Your father always looked and dressed like a tramp, anyhow. People remarked on it. So why worry? Natural causes! Fine. This way Amos will be dead and buried to everyone's satisfaction, and we will be free of him. No more questions or speculations from the villagers as to when he's coming back, or what's happened to him. Peace at last.' Her lips curved. 'And worth the price.'

'The price might be very high — for you. Suppose the real body is some day found? You'll be an accessory to murder. Had you thought of that?'

Elise shrugged. 'I'll worry about that if, or when, it happens.' She cast him a smile. 'Am I ever likely to? Have to worry about it, I mean? Where is he? I think you'd better tell me.'

He weighed his reply, then said: 'In Drearden's Wood. Over to the far north. A wild, tangled, untrodden tract there.' His teeth showed briefly. 'He's not likely to be disturbed.'

'Fair enough.' She shot him a curious glance. 'You've not been back there?'

'No. Dangerous, don't they say, for a murderer to return to the scene of the crime? I nearly did, though,' he admitted with sudden honesty, 'when that corpse was found in the quarry. I felt like bolting out of the back door and away, to check. But there just wasn't time.' After a short reflective silence, he said, in a cautious tone: 'How long had that tramp's body been in the car? How long dead?'

'Several days.' Catching the flicker in his eyes, the sudden tension, she added quickly: 'It's all right. I know Amos disappeared way back in April, but everyone will believe he went walkabout for a while, and that he was on his way home again when he stopped off in the quarry. No one is going to question the time of his death.' She was very conscious of his bounding relief.

With deliberate fingers, she untied her dressing-gown, tossed it aside. Stood.

Seth regarded her in silence, jaw set, then said roughly: 'Come to bed.' And his hot, glittering gaze held more command than invitation.

'You ask so irresistibly,' grinned Elise, removing his supper-tray to the bedside table and climbing between the sheets beside him. 'How can I refuse? However, there is one more little problem that I think you should know about before you take your lustful pleasure.' She slapped away his clutching hands. 'Kathie.'

'Kathie? What's the matter with Kathie, then?'

'She's pregnant.'

'Pregnant!' He rolled away from her and leaned up on one elbow to stare at her with horrified eyes. 'Are you sure?'

Elise nodded. 'I took her to see the doctor. She's been sick and seedy and out-of-sorts. And he confirmed it. About as far gone as I am. I'm afraid you didn't get to Amos fast enough, Seth.'

'But — '

'Oh, I don't mean that time you found him with her at Christmas. No. It must have been much later, round about April, I imagine. Just before you took a knife to him. Almost his last damned act on earth.' She frowned. 'He must have been making quite a habit of it.'

'Is that what Kathie says?' he asked whitely.

'It's what she told the doctor.' And half the waiting-room, she might have added, recalling Kathie's tearfully raised tones as she countered all the probing questions. 'Seth, she couldn't complain to you. She knew what you'd do, and what had

130

happened that one time when you did. Amos nearly crippled you . . . ' She saw his face, the lips clamped in a thin hard line, the grey-green eyes suddenly frighteningly flecked with ice. 'But you did know, didn't you?' she whispered slowly and, she thought, enlightened. 'That last time, you did know. And that's why you had to kill him!'

Seth lowered his head into his hands. 'What a goddamned mess,' he groaned.

'It could be worse. We'll cope. At least Amos is known to be dead, and soon to be buried. Kathie will receive nothing but sympathy, you'll see. Poor ill-treated, misused child.'

'That's it,' he said bleakly, glancing up. 'She is only a child. Fifteen. What does she know about looking after babies? Can't she get rid of it?'

'Abortion, you mean? That was suggested to her — tentatively. After all, what Amos did was nothing short of rape.' Elise gave a twisted smile. 'But — ' She shrugged. It was for Kathie to decide.

Something to call her own? Something

to love? It seemed that way. Understandable, if not sensible.

Seth scowled. 'I'll speak to her.'

'And twist her arm? . . . I wouldn't, Seth. The doctor says she's walking a very fine line, mentally. Pressure might just tip her over. Give it a day or two, anyhow.' Putting her arms about him she hugged his thin frame to her. 'Who, knowing the truth, could possibly blame you for acting as you did? A knife was far too good for him. May he rot in hell!'

'Amen, to that.'

Elise glanced down at her husband's dark head, resting against her just beneath her chin. Not much of his father in him, she'd say. Yet marked.

She said slowly: 'Why did Amos call you spawn of the Devil? Surely he didn't suspect your mother of being unfaithful to him, did he?'

'God, no. She'd never have dared . . . No. It was much more simple. Primitive, in fact. Fear.' He grinned faintly. Wriggling up against the pillows, he stretched over and, first removing the crockery, placed the empty supper-tray in front of her upon the bed. 'Watch.' He laid a spoon diagonally across the centre of the tray, leaned back against the pillows and deliberately folded his hands away behind his head.

Before her eyes, the spoon writhed and bent as if by its own volition.

Elise stared at the piece of twisted metal incredulously, then at him.

'You did that?'

He nodded. 'Seems a somewhat useless gift.'

'Is it difficult for you?'

'No. Takes a bit of concentration, that's all.'

He demonstrated again, this time with a fork, and from even further across the room. There was no question of his being able to touch the article.

'So that was why . . . ?' said Elise softly. She picked up the distorted fork and the metal parted in her hand.

'Yep. That art — if art is what you'd call it — drove Amos mad when I was a kid. He really thought it was a gift of the Devil; that I was cursed. And he did his best to beat it out of me. Oh, I used to retaliate — ' He smiled thinly. 'Twisting his digging fork under him, bending his keys, that kind of thing ... Until I learned the utter futility of riling him. It always made things so much worse for my mother and Kathie. They suffered vilely for any fleeting sense of satisfaction I might have had.' His mouth took on a grimmer line. 'I had an inkling that he might be right, too. That I really was some kind of freak. Some kind of Devil's spawn. Now, of course, I realize that metal-bending is not such a great oddity. At least, others have been recorded doing it. I'm not just one out on my own.' A flutter of smile in which relief still showed through. The child he had once been had suffered severe mental and physical mangling.

'Do you use your ... um ... talent often?'

'No. A bit pointless, isn't it? Besides — ' He threw her a rueful look. ' — I'm always afraid of others reacting in the way Amos did ... Best to stay quiet and keep my head down, wouldn't you say?' Gently, he took the pieces of mutilated fork from her fingers and dropped them onto the bedside table.

She grinned. 'And it could become expensive.'

But she understood, now, what had happened to the padlock at the watch-tower.

★   ★   ★

A week later, the body Elise had identified as that of Amos White was laid to rest in Chatton Eastwood churchyard, beside the unmarked grave of his long since ungrieving wife.

Later still, a headstone would be added. His name, and dates, and nothing more. R.I.P.

It was over.

9

Then, passionately — but fortunately without expertise — Kathie slashed her wrists.

Amos, it seemed, would continue to reach out from beyond the grave. For Seth . . . For Kathie . . .

Looking down at the childish face, the thin, bandaged wrists, Elise felt an overwhelming hatred for the man who had reduced this child to such despair.

Everyone, she thought bitterly, had suspected that Amos ill-treated his children; nobody had bothered to find out. To do anything. Herself, included. And now it was too late: all the damage had been done. Nothing left to do now but to pick up the pieces.

She caught back a sigh. 'Kathie,' she said gently, 'if you don't want to go through with this pregnancy, you have only to say so. Nobody is going to make you bear Amos' baby.'

'Go away,' said Kathie wearily, turning her eyes to gaze out of the window towards Drearden's Wood.

'No,' said Elise. 'You're still afraid of him, aren't you? After all these weeks, the thought of him still paralyses you with fear. But he's dead, Kathie. Gone. I promise you. He's in his grave.'

'Is he?'

'Yes. Amos is in his grave. And there are no ghosts, Kathie. No walking dead.' She studied the averted head. 'But this business about the child must be settled, one way or another. We can't just drift on, hoping the problem will go away.'

Kathie turned to face her. A small mocking smile curved her mouth. 'It's already settled, isn't it? Right here. Settled, and growing.' She flung back the bedcovers and folded her hands across her stomach. As yet, there was nothing to be seen. she was childishly flat, childishly immature. Her gaze flicked upwards. 'Are you getting rid of yours? Did Seth suggest that to you?'

'No, of course not.' Elise stared at her in shock. 'We want this child. Both of us.'

'Well, then.'

'Your situation is somewhat different.'

'Is it? What god-given right have you and yours to the universe, then?'

Elise stepped back, stung. After a moment she said quietly: 'Very well, Kathie. There's no more to be said. The choice is yours. Seth and I will do our best to make things easy for you, you know that. To back you up. Give you all the support we can — '

'That's big of you.'

Elise could have shaken her. Yet, at the same time, she felt desperately sorry for the child. Damn Amos.

'And . . . Kathie — ' Elise hesitated, wondering how far it was safe to go ' — it's not exactly a help to Seth, having you making . . . cat's cradles . . . in Drearden's Wood.'

The grey-green eyes that were very like Seth's flashed round to look at her, then slid away again.

'I don't know what you mean.' Kathie examined her finger-nails.

'Oh, I think you do.' A small gleam of amusement. 'We're fruits of the same great-granny — '

Away in the woods a cuckoo called, stammeringly, *cuck-cuck*, its cry already changing with the high season. The room was very warm, very still.

Elise said softly: 'And more danger to be had from the living than from the dead. Remember that,' She stared down at the bent head for a heartbeat longer, then turned and left the room. Enough hidden perils around, without Kathie compounding them. An idle comment from someone in the wrong quarter and . . .

She gave a slight cry and leaped backwards as a shadow lunged towards her from the doorway. Eyes wide, she stopped on discovering that the thickset black figure remained outlined in the oblong of sunlight.

Arthur Sullivan.

'What the hell do you think you're doing?' She glared at him, her heart still hammering in sickening thuds. 'You nearly frightened me to death.'

'Guilty conscience?'

'Get out.'

'Now, is that any way to greet a friend? Aren't you going to invite me in?'

'No. And if you try to force your way in, Seth will kill you.'

'Seth isn't here, is he?' he replied softly. 'Seth's doing a job at Langdons'.'

She opened her mouth to speak, closed it again. Useless to argue with him in his present mood, he'd obviously been drinking. Humour him.

'Come outside,' she said. 'Kathie's in there.' She jerked her head towards the inner downstairs room. 'I don't want her upset.'

She led him across a patch of sunlit grass.

'Now. What do you want?'

He considered her for several seconds, his head on one side. 'That's a brave question from one in your position.'

'I'm not afraid of you,' she said contemptuously.

'I can see that.' he leered towards her. 'But perhaps you ought to be . . . '

'If you put one finger on me, I'll — '

'I'm not going to touch you. Not yet, anyhow. And when I've finished what I've come for, you'll very likely do anything I ask.'

'And pigs might fly!'

'Very cocky, today, aren't we?' he grinned. 'But it might pay you to climb down from your high horse, Elise, before you get knocked down.' He jabbed a thumb towards the house. 'You're playing the wide-eyed fool with that one . . . Anyhow, I came here as an old pal, don't you forget that, to bring you a friendly warning . . . '

'Oh, get on with it, do.'

'I've heard that a piece of Drearden's Wood is to be sold. For building land.' He peered at her from small, cunning eyes to see how she was taking it. 'A few acres over to the north.'

'Who told you that?'

'Some mates of mine.'

'Didn't know you had any.'

'Well?'

'Well, what?'

'Rather upsets young Seth White's stinking fish-barrel, doesn't it?'

'I shouldn't think Seth'd care about it one way or the other,' said Elise loftily.

But her heart was hammering again, in heavy, sickened, frightened thuds. What did Arthur Sullivan know? What on earth *could* he know? Or was this all some kind of guessing game? Some trick to trip her up?

Arthur said, reflectively: 'I owed Amos a tenner. Was going to give it to him, too, only he never turned up. We'd arranged to meet at my place, one evening, on his way home from the Cow, over in Melhurst. Thrown out of the Jobbers' Arms, he'd been, after some New Year's revels there. Damned unfair, if you ask me. Banned him from the pub, they did . . . '

'I know that,' said Elise tightly.

'He used to take a short cut, to and from the Cow, through Drearden's Wood. Did you know that, too?' His voice was spiteful. 'Funny him going off suddenly like that.'

'Riotous.'

'And without first collecting his ten pounds. Odd, wouldn't you say?'

'Perhaps he forgot.'

'That's a joke! Amos?'

'Why haven't you told the police, then,

if it worries you?'

'What's in that for me?'

'Well, there's sure nothing due to you for telling me,' retorted Elise roundly.

'You think not?' His little eyes took on a cunning glint. 'You think about it, Elise. It might pay you to be nice to me — to be very nice to me, indeed, and make certain I keep my mouth shut. And I will. If it's made worth my while.' He leered. 'And I'm not talking only about money, girl, if you take my meaning.' He put his hand on her bare arm, ran it up and down in an exploratory fashion. Elise did not move. 'If you want to keep that skinny bed-bug of yours safe, you'd better think real hard. You see, I don't happen to believe that Amos White is lying peacefully in the churchyard. I don't happen to believe that that corpse, which was found so conveniently in the quarry, is Amos at all. More likely some old tramp.' He grinned. 'I warrant we'd find a whole lot of surprises under old Amos' headstone, if we were to investigate.'

'That's for the police to say,' said Elise, ashen-lipped. 'They'll not go digging up

Amos' grave on your say-so, anyhow.'

'Wouldn't need to, would they? Not at first. Likely better for them to try over in Drearden's Wood.'

'Why do you say that?' She tried to keep her voice steady and failed.

'Told you. I knew Amos' habits. If I put my mind to it, I could make a fair guess as to where he might be lying right now.'

'Then you'd better inform someone in authority, hadn't you?' said Elise, with a bravado she did not feel.

'You don't really mean that,' he said, grinning again. 'I'll give you a few days to think about it. To weigh the pros and cons. If you change your mind — and you will, if you have any fondness for that wet-behind-the-ears, titty-sucking kid husband of yours — I'll be up at Lethman's orchard. All day. In fact, I'll be there for the whole week, because I've some tree-thinning to do. So you can find me there. Any time.' He stretched his lips in an unpleasant smile. 'But I should make it pretty fast. I'm getting kinda horny, and if I'm not satisfied I might just let something slip.'

'Your axe, hopefully,' said Elise from between her teeth. 'Arthur Sullivan, you're a bastard, and if you think I'm going to come crawling to you . . . ' She stared at him with fury greening her eyes.

'Crawl you will,' he said softly. 'And soon. And don't you go trying any of your witch's tricks on me, either. Up to them, I am, and I've got my protection, see.' Elise watched him in disbelief as he scrabbled in his pocket and held up a bunch of cinquefoil. The creeping herb's yellow flowers were wilting sadly. 'You can't do anything with that around, can you? Plenty of that at my place, see.' He leered. 'You'll be dancing to my tune all right, see if you're not.'

'If I wanted to,' said Elise disdainfully, 'I could eat you for breakfast, and spit out the pips.'

For a few seconds he looked unsure, the bully in him sagging, and she saw his fingers grope towards his pocket. Then he rallied.

'There's one sure way to deal with witches,' he said.

'A stake through my heart, like they

thrust through Mercy Goodbright's?' sneered Elise. 'A lot of fun that'll be for you.'

'A stake's about right,' he snarled. 'But not the kind you're meaning, girl, and not through your soddin' little heart, either. Oh, dear me, no . . . '

'You're out of your tiny mind.'

'Underestimated old Arthur, didn't you? Fancied you could pick him up and then chuck him down whenever you felt like it . . . Well, you'll learn differently, now. So will Seth and young Kathie, if I'm not mistaken. And so will a whole heap of others. Your toffee-nosed Langdon chums, for a couple more. Plenty I could tell the world about those two. Like why they're so smarmily wrapped up in each other — ' He grabbed her wrist and twisted it sharply. 'So you can lay off the sheep's eyes there, girl: young Lance is otherwise occupied.'

'You're as daft as a brush,' gasped Elise.

'Ah, that's what Master Lance thinks, too,' said Arthur. 'He imagines old Arthur's thick as a brick; that I haven't tumbled to what he was up to that day at

Frognalls bridge. Part of the scenery, old Arthur . . . Slip him a fiver, and he'll lie drunk till noon.' He scowled. 'But I'm not so daft, not by a long chalk!' He gave her wrist another vicious twist.

Elise clenched her teeth against the pain. 'Oh, so you put on an act, do you?' she mocked.

'Very funny! And that's one more I owe you, girl.' He released her as abruptly as he had taken hold.

'Lethman's orchard. Be there!' He strode towards the gate, turned as he reached it. 'You tell young Seth, mind. Tell him what I've told you. Word for word. I'm sure he'll manage to persuade you where his interests lie.'

* * *

'Maybe I should pay a call on Arthur,' said Seth pleasantly, when Elise relayed the greater part of the conversation to him, keeping only the scurrilous allegations about the Langdons to herself. 'Now. Show him that he's not welcome around here.'

147

'No,' said Elise impatiently. 'Stay away from him, Arthur Sullivan's no problem.'

'No?' Seth's lips curved in amusement. 'You can deal with him, then?'

Elise stared at him.

'Arthur Sullivan,' prompted Seth. 'What had you in mind?' He smiled at her, and took her into his arms. 'I rather think I might object to you paying him in the required terms of his blackmail,' he said against her hair.

'Arthur Sullivan's getting nothing,' she said. 'Not even a black eye from you. He's not worth it.'

'Besides, it's not necessary.'

'No?'

'He's not going to go to the police, whatever we decide to do. That's all a lot of hot air on his part. He runs too many lawless little activities of his own . . . ' Seth grinned. 'I could tell you a thing or two about our Arthur . . . '

'So could I,' said Elise, feelingly.

'And he's not likely to get policemen digging up the graveyard, believe me. The worst he can do now is whisper in one or two ears, and that's all it will be

— vindictive whispers. And treated as such. No one around here is going to exhume Amos on friend Arthur's say-so.'

'No — ' Elise bit her lip. 'There's only one danger — '

Seth stood her away from him and looked at her inquiringly.

'Drearden's Wood, you mean?'

She nodded. 'He might possibly get someone interested enough to sniff about there. I doubt it, but it's a chance, and he insists he could make a good stab at pointing out Amos' true burial spot.'

'And do you think he can?'

'Do you?' she countered.

'If he really knows the route Amos took home from the pub in Melhurst, then, yes,' said Seth slowly. 'The likeliest spot for an ambush and the nearest one to the densest undergrowth; I didn't want to have to drag Amos' body for miles . . . ' He gave a slight sigh. 'It seems reasonable to suppose Arthur'd work that out for himself. Damn!' His brow furrowed. 'I didn't realize that anybody knew my father's path home, least of all, Arthur — it was my old man's own, not a regular trackway; hardly marked — '

'I don't relish the sound of the rest of his story, either,' said Elise. 'The idea that part of the property's being sold for a housing development. Bulldozers'd churn up anything.'

'Not much we can do about that. Probably years before the whole thing's settled, anyhow. Bound to be plenty of opposition to the scheme from various quarters.' He frowned. 'I wonder why the old sod didn't speak sooner.'

'Ten pounds,' said Elise. 'Free in his pocket ... But blackmail now comes sweeter.' She went on, in a determined tone: 'However, there's a way to scotch Arthur's little blackmailing enterprise and make everything safe, once and for all. Now.'

'How?'

'Move Amos' body.'

'No,' whispered Seth. 'I can't.'

'Put him where he belongs, under his headstone in the churchyard.'

'No,' whispered Seth again, his face ashen. 'I can't. You don't know what you're asking. He'll be ... ' His voice trailed off and he gazed at her in horror.

'There are plenty of rubbish-sacks; he can be wrapped in plastic,' said Elise, inexorably.

'I . . . can't.'

'Then I can.' She stared across at him. 'If I have to.'

'No! No,' said Seth. 'Not you. I can't let you . . . ' He shuddered. 'I'll do it. I'll move him.' but he wasn't sure how he'd stand it. Rotting flesh and vile putrescence — even from the grave Amos'd break him. He moistened his lips.

'We'll both move him,' said Elise. 'I doubt if you've planted him six feet deep, and the graveyard soil won't yet be hard as iron. It can all be done in a night. We'll need a wheelbarrow or truck or something. And tools.'

'You'd not get anything on wheels through that area.'

'I've seen gypsies hauling a four-wheeled cart through there. Loaded, it was . . . It broke an axle,' she said reflectively.

'Christ, that's bloody encouraging.'

'We could use a kind of *travois* — a

wheelless contraption which is pulled from one end.'

'We could sling him between two poles and carry him,' said Seth with bitter sarcasm.

'The North American Indians once dragged *travois* along behind them.'

'Did they now? Well, well. And probably on some dirty great Plain, not through the matted underbrush of Drearden's damned Wood.'

'You're just looking for complications.'

'You're right.'

'Seth — '

'Suppose someone sees us? It would be suicide.'

'Then we must make sure that nobody does see.'

'The churchyard can hardly be locked and curtained,' said Seth despairingly. 'And there's Kathie . . . '

'Your sister can spend a few days with Mrs Goode; Ruby'd be delighted to have her. Stop making problems. No one's likely to be interested in Chatton Eastwood's graveyard at three-thirty in the morning.'

'You'd be surprised! . . . All right, all right,' he said hastily, as her eyes flashed out at him. 'I'll move him. I'll bloody well move him. But it's going to be difficult.'

'Not as difficult as you think,' said Elise, her arms going round him. 'You'll see.'

10

Bevan Oake stood in the doorway of the Whites' cottage and glanced around him. Tidier, he noted, than when he had last seen it. And cleaner. The sun shafted hot across his neck and shoulders and made gleaming puddles on the red-tiled floor. He hadn't wanted to come. Imperative, though, that he did so. He raised his eyes to the golden-green inspection of Elise's. She hadn't been to the rectory for more than a week and he wondered why. No message. No explanation. No call. Unreliable, Mrs Pawcett had said. Well, maybe so. But that was not the reason why he was at the cottage. Difficult, though, to broach the subject tactfully, and he was shaken by the change in her. She looked unwell, pale and drawn, and with huge dark shadows around her lovely eyes. Drained. All the warm, butterfly brightness gone. God, what was the lad doing to her?

His gaze travelled scorchingly across to Seth, who was standing silently in the background. He, too, looked as if the wedded state was not working totally to his advantage. Thinner than ever, and greyly pale, there was a strained expression around his mouth and eyes. Of course, thought Bevan, there'd been all that recent trouble with Kathie . . .

For a moment longer, the rector studied the gaunt face before him. It appeared so young. Defenceless. The features wearing the closed aspect of a person in a trance, the eyes blank, seeing nothing but the devils within. Bevan threw him a narrow smile. But there was no answering movement of the other's lips. The boy's leaden eyes stared out at him, haunted, hagridden and not young at all.

Maybe the unpleasantness of Amos's untimely death — ? But — surely, a blessing in disguise? That difficult old man, in his grave. Bevan gave a strangled sigh. So, back to that again; no way of introducing his subject with any kind of tact, or he could not think of any.

'I'm very sorry,' he said baldly, 'but I'm afraid I have to tell you that your father's grave has been tampered with . . . '

He had expected consternation, disbelief, even. But not this combined outgush of — fear, was it? The dread-filled atmosphere swirled about him almost tangibly. He saw Elise flash an apprehensive glance towards Seth. The boy looked sicker than ever, or as if he'd seen a ghost. He was literally swaying on his feet. Elise moved swiftly across to hold his arm. To keep him upright Bevan guessed.

'My husband's not been too fit,' she said. 'The strain of the last weeks — ' Mind, strength and will had been taxed to the limit of endurance: Seth could take no more. But what to do? Her teeth gnawed on her lip.

'No — ' said Bevan hurriedly. 'No. Please don't distress yourselves. Clumsy of me, I know, breaking the news in such an ugly fashion. It's all right. Nothing's been vandalised. No act of outright desecration or anything like that, you understand — Even the flowers are still there. A little . . . disturbance, no more. It was just that, when I heard the rumours, I went round to check, and noticed that the soil there had been freshly moved — '

'I'd done a bit of digging,' said Elise faintly. 'I was going to plant some primroses.'

'I don't think it was that,' said Bevan, troubled. 'It looked rather . . . hurried. Furtive, even.' He stood, looking unhappy.

'You said 'rumours',' prompted Elise. 'What kind of rumours?'

'For a while now there's been a certain amount of . . . um . . . unrest in the parish, and vague stories of clandestine meetings in the graveyard, and the odd unexplained dead cock, and suchlike — '

'Ah,' said Elise, light dawning. 'The rumblings of witchcraft, or devil-worship, or whatever.' She looked suddenly released, almost radiant. 'Has all that started up again?'

The rector gave a rueful smile. 'Does it ever stop in some of these rural districts?'

'I doubt it.' Elise grinned buoyantly. 'The Devil's an easy master.'

'Well,' said Bevan, 'it's probably all a bit of a storm in a teacup, you know what people are . . . A handful of feathers and someone will turn it into a full-blown orgy — '

'Oh, I'm aware of that,' replied Elise, her voice lilting. 'I've lived here all my life. There's nothing that would surprise me about the folk of Chatton Eastwood.'

'No, I expect not.' Like Arthur Sullivan and his depressing bunches of cinquefoil, counterparts of which had been frozen forever into oaken stillness by some long forgotten ancestor in the church. Superstition hadn't changed much, reflected Bevan. 'However, I wanted to stifle these present rumours as soon as possible, before they grew out of all proportion, and I thought I ought to have a word with you, because, well — ' He hesitated. 'Amos is our most recent burial, and there are evidently certain misguided souls who might see fit to take advantage of that fact. In their . . . evil practices.' He gave a distasteful grimace.

'Ah . . . ' murmured Elise slowly. 'I see . . . '

'Some people, too, who will spread . . . um . . . wild stories.' He had no intention of telling either Elise or Seth about the interview he had had with Arthur Sullivan. The man was a trouble-maker and a fool. And his latest accusation only served to show that he was thoroughly unbalanced in his attitude to the Whites ... It had taken Bevan some time to appreciate Arthur's point, mainly because the man had been too drunk to make it. Elise had put a spell on him, indeed! But there were some who would believe it ...

Bevan's smile was wry. 'I didn't wish you to hear some garbled version of the disturbance at the churchyard, and be upset.'

'No,' said Elise gravely. She guided him towards the door. 'Thank you.'

Stepping out into the sunshine, she turned. 'I expect it was some animal scratching around, attracted by the bare soil. Seth and I must have the grave turved.'

It was only as she spoke her husband's name, that Bevan realized Seth had not uttered one single word.

He opened the gate. 'You could be

right,' he said, going through. With a twitch of the latch, he closed the gate again and stood facing her across it. 'There was definitely someone in the churchyard, though. Very late. My brother, Jonathan, saw lights. He sleeps poorly, and prowls the house — ' Seeing her automatic, disbelieving start, he smiled and elucidated: 'In his wheelchair.'

'Oh, I see . . . And he didn't call you to investigate?'

Bevan shook his head. 'I rather gather he was on the side of the night-time prowlers,' he said, with a faint rueful curve to his lips. He thought, although he did not say so, that Jonathan would be on the side of anyone or anything that threatened to discomfort his brother.

Elise put out her hand to him across the gate, and he took it in his, slender and suntanned and warm.

'Thank you for coming,' she said formally, but with an uptilt of her head and a sudden glinting green smile from those familiar-looking, wide eyes between their sweep of lashes. Invitation? Encouragement?

Bevan glanced down, disconcerted. Shapely bare brown legs, tapering to narrow ankles . . . no help for his confusion there. He looked away; up . . . spotted her bracelet with unconcealed relief.

'Jet, isn't it?' he asked quickly. 'A queer stone — The ancients believed it had magical powers.' Lifting her arm carefully, he examined the ornament. 'Did you know that it becomes magnetic when rubbed?' He ran the ball of his thumb across her wrist.

'It was my grandmother's,' said Elise, gently removing her hand from his. She swung the heavy black lumps on their silver chains. 'It's not really valuable, but I like the sensation of it against my arm. It feels . . . at home.' She smiled up at him again, a siren's smile, the sun tipping the curve of her lips with fire. He yearned to bend over and press his mouth to hers. So long, he thought, since he'd enjoyed a woman's warmth. Then savoured the uncomfortable possibility that he was being led.

'I must go,' he said hurriedly. A spellbinder, indeed. Arthur Sullivan had said as much. Nonsense, of course. As was all that stuff about her grandmother having been a witch and flown from the watchtower; but he wondered what had really given rise to that old story. It would interest him to know.

'Are you going straight home now?' Her teeth showed, very white and even. 'If so, perhaps you'd care to take some cherries back with you?' She gestured behind her to the laden cherry tree.

'No,' he said regretfully. 'I've several more ports of call.' He hesitated before shooting her a grin. 'I'll have a raincheck on the cherries, though.'

'Any time.'

He stood looking down at her, then said: 'Arthur Sullivan's suffered a slight accident, had you heard? His axe slipped and caught his shin a nasty gash.' Elise to blame, Arthur'd said.

Her eyes flickered momentarily, a flash of gold across the green, but all she said was: 'Oh, dear.'

'Yes. I shall look in on him later, take him a couple of paperbacks ... ' He patted his pocket.

'Tea and sympathy. How kind.' A spreading grin that answered his own, her bright gaze squarely on his face.

'Samaritan.' His eyes slid away, and he turned to walk reluctantly from her along the carttrack.

Elise watched him go.

So the rector believed there was black magic abroad, did he? She followed his progress down the track with a smile touching the corners of her mouth.

She wasn't sure about Arthur Sullivan, but it would be relatively easy to bewitch the Reverend Oake . . .

★   ★   ★

Darkness was falling by the time Bevan pointed his toes towards home. A long day, he thought wearily, but one spent in good company, on the whole. And a very pleasant meal to conclude it. He contemplated the Langdons with affection. Excellent food and splendid wine. Mrs Pawcett's repasts left much to be desired, as did Jonathan's conversation.

Swinging to his right, he took the path

that led through some woods and then through the yew-girt churchyard, in a short cut to the rectory. It was dark under the trees and he had no torch, but here and there moon and starshine filtered down in moving silver patches, so that there was sufficient light to see his way. Once, nearing the end of his journey, he paused beside a gravestone, peering down. A dark slab, with darker letters incised upon it. A child's grave. Recent. He could not read it in the dimness, but he knew who lay there; knew who rested beneath each one of those carefully carved stones. Knew the names, if not the people. Only the unmarked graves confused him. Who slept here? And here? Brow creased, he stared intently at the mounded grass.

The church bulked in front of him, black against a lighter sky, the sturdy Norman tower a bite across the stars; a reassuring edifice that possessed no great beauty, but remained a squat and solid statement of faith in enduring, hand-cut stone. A light glimmered greyly from its leaded windows.

Bevan frowned.

Eleven o'clock, or thereabouts? Who could be within?

Feet silent on the damp grass, he walked across to the west door. Opened it.

Heavy stillness met him. There was no one there.

Only a black candle burning on the altar.

With a hiss of anger, Bevan crossed to snuff it out. These childish posturings, he thought grimly, were going too far.

A slight sound made him turn.

There was a figure in the doorway, cloaked and hooded and glowing eerily.

Bevan was far from scared by this apparition.

It would take more than some crazy villager dressed in a cowled habit to rattle him, thought the rector crossly, thrusting the black candle into his pocket and bounding down the aisle at an unecclesiastical gallop.

Accelerating forward, he almost reached the door as the monkishly-clad form whirled to flee. Bevan lunged, clutching, and grasped rushing air, and, for a second, the hem of the cloak with the fingers of one hand. But a good tight hold on the fabric eluded him, and his momentum threw him headlong, pitching him temporarily to his knees. All he was left with in his hand was a tiny fragment of something hard. He dragged himself upright. Went forward again, out into the night.

The racing figure was already far from him and obviously knew the area better than he. It headed away from the rectory, away from the church and gravestones, into the surrounding trees, and was soon lost among the undergrowth of the encircling wood.

Bevan stopped and listened. Nothing. Neither crack of twigs nor rustle of footfall. Only the sighing of the breeze in the tops of the trees. And the moon and stars above him.

And, in his hand, the torn fragment glowing, a ghostly bluish-white.

11

'It's touchwood,' said Cade Burrell, picking up the object the rector held out on the palm of his hand. 'Rotten timber infected by the honey fungus. Makes good kindling. It also glows in the dark.' In the bright morning sunlight, the sliver Bevan had wrenched from the night-visitant's cloak lay grey and dead-looking. 'The toadstool's a parasite. Kills trees.' The countryman leaned the axe he had been wielding against a pile of freshly-cut fencing posts and turned the fragment over in his fingers. 'See. Those black threads under the bark . . . ? They're from the fungus; they attack the wood and cause the odd phosphorescence . . . ' He raised his head. 'Where did you find it?'

Bevan told him where — and how.

'Interesting,' commented Cade dryly.

Bevan gave a slight smile. 'As you say.' He hesitated for a moment or two, staring down at the now inoffensive-looking touchwood in his friend's hand. Then said: 'Is it used in witches' sabbats?'

'Not to my knowledge,' returned Cade. 'But I'm no expert on such matters. Could well be.' He grinned. 'Useful stuff, I'd say, if one fancies a touch of the weirdies. I know they used to light the old smugglers' paths with it through the bogs. Probably what gave rise to a lot of the tales about travellers being led astray by fairies and hobgoblins.' He laughed. 'The children around here collect it for Hallowe'en. It makes a satisfyingly eerie glow in the darkness if gummed around one's clothes. I remember doing that, years ago, with — ' He stopped abruptly. That might be telling tales out of school. 'We were about twelve or thirteen, I remember,' he went on, 'and we scared the pants off old Drummond Innes. Possibly your unwelcome visitor was one of the children, up to tricks.'

'I don't think so,' said Bevan. He was pretty sure that the figure had been no child. Neither, he thought, had it had the weight and bearing of a man. A woman, then? He smiled crookedly. He'd rather run out of options. Definitely a woman, then. But who? And — more important — why?

'Come and share my sandwiches,' invited Cade, indicating a massive lunch-box reposing on a tree-stump. 'I'm due for a break, and you'll not be depriving me; there's enough in there to feed a horse.'

Bevan accepted readily. He had arrived intending to mention Arthur Sullivan's preposterous tales about certain and various members of his parish, and to elicit Cade's views on those, also. Cade knew the village and its inhabitants; his advice would be sound, and anything said between the two of them would go no further. A quiet man who said little and kept himself to himself, he was one of the few people with whom the rector could hold a conversation without feeling that he was being measured and found wanting. Diffident himself, rather than outgoing, Bevan was being forced to question more and more these days just what had made him choose his particular vocation, and he found himself becoming increasingly irritated by his parishioners' petty problems and pressures. Things had been different when Julie had been alive. She had kept him on an even keel and held all the trivial pinpricks of life at bay. He was only now beginning to appreciate the payload she must have carried, without complaint, and without his having, seemingly, even noticed.

Sighing inwardly, he held out his hand for the bread and cheese offered to him, and bit into it reflectively.

The woods were very quiet, an oasis of green peace, dense-leaved with summer. Only now and again the stillness was momentarily shattered by the harsh, jangling cry of a jay, deep among the trees. The clearing where the two men sat eating their sandwiches was full of sun and the scent of newly-cut timber. Wood chippings strewed the ground about their feet.

Bevan wondered if his self-contained, dark-eyed companion felt any stabs of past disappointments, or if the solitude had long since healed all grievances. All pain. The hurts from Michael Goode?

From Elise? What had happened there? ... And there? Something not to be asked, not even by a friend.

In affable silence, the two men sat side by side on a fallen treetrunk in the sunshine, each busy with his own thoughts. Each, had they but known it, returning again and again in ever decreasing circles to a constant, common problem. Arthur Sullivan.

*   *   *

Arthur Sullivan himself was, at that moment, limping his way back along the driveway that led from Langdon House. He was in a foul temper, stone-cold sober — and lacking the wherewithal to remedy that painful condition — and in considerable discomfort from the cut on his shin, which had not been improved by his decision to take that morning's — abortive — hike. Muttering angrily to himself, and slashing with his stick at the overgrown verges as he walked, the gist of his running soliloquy appeared to be that *someone was going to pay* ...

Lance Langdon watched him go.

The chiselled face was expressionless under the sun, the hair a glinting golden helmet which never stirred. For long minutes, only the eyes in that motionless head moved, adjusting themselves to the slow progess of the dwindling figure along the drive. The stick beating at the creamy surf of meadowsweet left a faint haze of dust and pollen dancing in its wake and, on the warm air, a drifting summer sweetness.

'What did *he* want?' asked Theda, coming forward and taking her brother by the arm.

'He was trying a spot of blackmail, I think,' said Lance. Cold blue eyes swivelled to stare into eyes of an equally cold, bright blue.

'I hope you sent him off with a flea in his ear?'

'I did that.' Lance squeezed forth a thin smile. 'Although I'm not too sure that it was the best thing to do. Maybe I should have given him something. I can't guess what trouble the damned fellow's going to cause.'

'Arthur Sullivan's life's work is causing trouble,' replied Theda easily. 'So, what's new? Someday, someone's going to shut his big mouth for good . . . And I, for one, will dance on his grave.'

'Then say your prayers that it's soon.'

Theda looked quickly at her brother. 'You're serious? It's as bad as that?' She studied his face, traced a hand across his cheek. 'You really are worried, aren't you? What's the old devil been up to?'

'He saw me with the Land-Rover, down by Frognalls bridge . . . Or so he says.'

Theda's breath drew in on a hiss. 'Way back in April, you mean?'

Lance nodded.

'I told you at the time that it was a mistake to move the boy.' Theda's blue eyes had narrowed. 'It was stupid.'

'What was I supposed to do? Leave him there? . . . And what would have happened when the police decided to poke around? A great help that would have been to us, Sis, wouldn't it?'

'All the same, dumping him where you did, sooner or later somebody was bound to start asking questions — like, why was the child on the Hatchins road, anyhow?'

'I did the most sensible thing, if you could but see it,' insisted Lance obstinately. 'And without too much time to plan anything. The walls along Hatchins are built of the same stone as those by Frognalls, so less likelihood of having awkward questions asked. If I'd just tipped him into any old ditch — ' His arm came round the girl's shoulder, held her close.

' — They might have found Frognalls' stone in his hair or clothes,' she finished for him. 'I suppose so.' She stared along the now empty drive. 'Did Arthur actually spot you with the boy?'

'No ... I don't know ... ' He shrugged. 'He may have done.'

'How?'

'I have no idea. There was no one there. At least, I saw no one,' said Lance. 'Maybe he didn't see me. Maybe he's just guessing — '

'Oh, yes,' returned Theda, with bitter sarcasm. 'That's really something he could manage to make an educated guess about, isn't it? What did Arthur, in fact, allege?'

'That he'd seen me parked with the Land-Rover, by Frognalls bridge, on a certain very interesting day in April.'

'And that was all?'

'More or less. It was enough, wasn't it? And I could hardly ask him outright if he'd seen me touch the boy. Regrettably, there was nothing much I could say, without dropping myself deeper into the mess. I had to footsie-tootsie round the subject, pretending I was completely in the dark, hoping he'd give me a clue to how much he'd found out. I think — ' said Lance slowly ' — that he knows rather a lot. More than is good for us, anyhow. And not only about Robin Goode, I'd say. I may be wrong. But something he said — ' He glanced down at his sister. 'About how we'd soon be in the money . . .'

'That's ridiculous. How *could* he know? We were so careful — ' Theda looked suddenly frightened. 'We'll have to do something quickly.'

'Easier said than done, little sister.' He kissed the crown of her shining hair. 'With all these snags and holdups, we must possess ourselves in patience.'

'Quickly! Or we'll lose everything.'

'Sis,' he said patiently, 'I can't just trundle the damned stuff off into the wild blue yonder. We have to wait. Until Symo's ready.'

'He was supposed to *be* ready. What the hell is he playing at!'

'It's important not to lose our heads; we mustn't be panicked into doing something foolish.'

'Who's panicking? And if anyone's going to lose his damned head it's going to be Arthur Sullivan, not me,' said Theda viciously. 'So he'd better watch it. Scabby-mouthed creep.'

She turned away, tugging on her brother's arm, and they meandered together across the daisy-spattered grass towards the house.

Bevan Oake was already there, standing on the stretch of shaggy lawn, the gloss of his shoes dusted over with pollen. He appeared to be staring broodingly at the heavy, frontal scowl of the building before him.

'Ugly, isn't it?' said Theda, with a silvery laugh, as she came up to him. 'Dark, damp and depressing.'

Bevan rounded, smiling. 'Nothing a little judicious renovation couldn't cure.'

'And the resident ghost?'

'Does she walk?'

'So they say. Ask Lance.' She laughed up at her brother and Bevan thought what a handsome couple they made; strong, straight and golden. Theda was about the most beautiful girl he had ever seen. But she stirred absolutely nothing in him, unless it was a skip of the heart at such pure perfection. She could have been quite sexless, a lovely ornament, for all the physical reaction she drew from him. He pondered, for a moment, the inequalities and mysteries of sex. What was the magical ingredient that could make one person attractive to another; which could — because of it, and for it — win empires, lose kingdoms? He'd loved his wife, Julie, in that kind of soul-searing fashion. And, after her death, the fire had gone out. It was only recently that . . .

He shook himself, saw Lance staring at him, a smile on his arrogantly-carved lips.

'You're far from us, Rector,' he teased. 'Composing next Sunday's sermon?'

Bevan gave a sheepish grin. 'It's the effect this place has; I was carried away by my own thoughts . . . Elise's grandmother worked here, didn't she?'

'That's right.' Lance threw him an amused glance. 'I take it you've heard the village gossip about her flying from the watchtower?'

A cautious smile curved Bevan's mouth.

'What's your version? That she jumped?'

'Of course the stupid woman jumped. Her body was never found because someone picked her up and buried her.'

'Sounds plausible,' murmured Bevan, his eyes still on the house.

Lance said smoothly: 'People were only too willing to sanction all that poppycock about flying because her mother was Mercy Goodbright, the sometime-resident, so-called witch, who, by then, had already been messily skewered by the locals. And the same thing was said about *her*. That she could fly. Not that anyone actually saw her; not in the air, I mean. But she *said* she could fly, and the village believed her. Too terrified to do otherwise, if you ask me. She evidently led them a merry jig, one way and another. Anyhow, she was once shut in the old watchtower — the lookout room was used at one time as the local lock-up for mild misdemeanours — with doors bolted top and bottom and no way out except straight down to the rocks below . . . whumph! Yet, the next minute, there she was strutting the streets as bold as brass and claiming that she'd flown.' He grinned. 'Having that tale stuffed up her jumper ensured Elise's grannie of a certain immediate immortality when she chose to launch off the way she did.'

'You think someone took advantage of the older story?'

Lance shrugged. 'Pretty obvious, isn't it? Though I don't know what they'd got to gain. Anyhow, it seems it was the girl's own fault. According to my father she encouraged everybody to believe that she had the same supernatural powers as her mother was said to have had — Trickery, or not, there's no smoke without fire, as the saying goes, and the village was convinced of it.'

'Poor girl,' said Bevan with compassion. 'It couldn't have been much of a life for her after losing her mother in that terrible fashion.' He frowned. 'And why do folk never give her a name? It's always 'Elise's grandmother' or, worse still, 'Mercy Goodbright's daughter'. Hardly a barrel of laughs, that one. Had she no identity of her own?'

Lance gave a twisted grin. 'It would scarcely have helped her,' he said dryly. 'She was called Mercy, after her mother, and later married a Goodbright cousin . . . '

Theda's laugh tinkled across them.

'You'll soon find out that everyone's related to everyone else around here, on both sides of the blanket, Bevan dear, so tread softly. If you insult one, you'll insult them all.'

'I'll be careful to guard my tongue,' promised Bevan. He cast an apologetic glance at her. 'I only looked in to thank your father for the dinner invitation — I hope he remembered to tell you?' Lawrence Langdon was notorious for forgetting everything of less than earth-shattering importance.

'He did mumble something in passing,' grinned Theda.

'Your father tossed a note in at the rectory this morning, but I missed him, and I didn't seem able to reach him by telephone.'

'Phone's off the hook,' said Lance laconically.

'He's arranging his butterflies,' explained Theda. 'Shall I tell him you're here?' He wouldn't welcome it. She grimaced. 'Unfortunately, one of the display cabinets was smashed when we had that burglary, and he's been trying to salvage the remains ever since.'

'Then don't disturb him,' said Bevan. 'I'll see him tonight. I shall be delighted to come for dinner — yet again.' His voice held mischief. 'Mrs Pawcett's having one of her economy drives.'

'It seems Father's going to be disturbed, whether he likes it or not,' remarked Lance, his eyes on a large, covered lorry trundling towards them along the drive. 'Here's his wood.'

'Wood?' echoed Bevan faintly, his gaze going to where a myriad trees curtseyed and beckoned beyond the shrubbery.

Theda pulled a face. 'Nothing so commonplace as homegrown,' she murmured. 'This is mahogany, no less. Lawrence insisted. Planed and polished, first-grade material for his wall-panels and shelving — to replace the stolen tapestries. It's costing a fortune.'

The lorry ground to rest.

'I'll attend to it,' said Lance, and strode away from them.

Bevan, too, turned to leave, then swung back.

'You've heard nothing hopeful about your missing treasures, then?'

'No. And not likely to, I'd guess. Whoever lifted those wall-hangings must have had a ready buyer. The stuff's probably on its way to America by now.'

'A pity. I feel very strongly,' said Bevan pompously, 'that such heirlooms should remain in their home and country environment.'

Theda gave a hoot of laughter. 'Bevan, dear, you're absolutely priceless. What tall, ivory tower did you step from? Doubtless the things were plundered from some foreign shore by some long-ago Langdon, in the first place.'

'Then you don't regret losing them?' asked Bevan in a stiff tone.

'Only the money they might one day have been expected to bring,' replied Theda with laughing honesty. 'They're difficult to insure and even harder to care for, and a couple of right miserable scenes, to boot. The Sacrifice of Isaac, and The Expulsion from Eden. How would you like those glumping over your cornflakes?' She arched golden brows. 'Anyhow, there's precious little left. When Father dies, death duties will swallow the rest. The house will have to be sold. There's no money for its upkeep; I imagine someone will buy the place and pull it down. Build a dogs' home, or an estate of brick boxes . . . '

Bevan stared at her, aghast. 'And that

doesn't upset you?'

Blue eyes danced at him. 'No. Am I too awful? Lance and I have lived all our lives in this mouldering mausoleum; you can't really believe that we'd grieve over it?'

'Does Lance feel as you do?'

'Of course.' She stretched her arms, rose on her toes, her lovely face lifted towards the sky. 'Freedom. To walk forever in the sun.' Her laugh tinkled out again at the sight of Bevan's shocked expression. 'The days of wine and roses are over, Bevan dear. The time of the stately home is finished and gone with the era of cheap and willing servants, and it will never return. And I'm not prepared to shoulder this household more or less single-handed for the rest of my life. There's more to existence than cleaning and polishing and preserving — and shoring up a crumbling estate upon which no one wishes to work, and couldn't be paid if they did.'

Her voice took on an undercurrent of bitterness.

'Lance feels the same way. Neither of us can recall the place in its heyday, anyway; neither of us has any fond memories; it has all been scrape and pinch and grind for as long as we can remember. And Father . . . ' She frowned, suddenly silent.

Bevan could guess at her thoughts, there. Any slight increase in the flow of the financial stream would always have been channelled in Lawrence Langdon's own direction. Charming, autocratic and completely self-centred, it would never have occurred to him that his children might have separate and different needs.

Bevan smiled. 'A pity you can't find your missing diamond,' he said.

'Oh, you've heard about that, too, have you?' chuckled Theda.

'With embellishments.'

She chuckled again. 'You would. It's the village's standing mystery, their *pièce de résistance*. Their answer to every other chronicle of hidden gold or buried treasure. And, by golly, one day, who knows..?'

Bevan's face creased with responding humour. 'But why,' he queried softly, 'did Elise's grandmother choose to curse your wretched bauble in the first place?'

'To hit back at the Langdon family. What else? She was married, and had been carrying on a backdoor liaison with the — then — rector. A randy young goat, if one credits the reports. Anyhow, Langdon (— great-grandfather Langdon, that was —) found out and took her to task, made the usual threats of exposure and loss of good name and the parson's living, I imagine, and the affair was terminated. Hushed up. After her death, no one seems to have paid any more attention to the rector's lapse — if they had ever known of it, that is.'

'Too busy branding her as a witch,' said Bevan dryly.

'True. Anyhow, her sweetheart, the rector, appears to have lived out the rest of his days in undeserved tranquillity; married a girl from Melhurst and produced seven children. So the little Goodbright's timely flight scotched any scandal there.'

'Providential,' growled Bevan. 'Attention focused firmly on something. altogether more newsworthy.' And he wondered if that sly man of the cloth had also shown a dexterous hand with a shovel. He looked across at Theda. 'It beats me why your revered ancestors didn't lock their precious diamond in a decent, foolproof strongbox — two or three strongboxes, if necessary, in a barred and securely locked room. Would have saved a lot of bother. And to hell with '*and no safe will be able to hold it*'!'

The bright-haired girl at his side gave him back a measuring stare. 'They did,' she said. 'Several times. They used the strongest, most foolproof safes money could buy. Locked doors and barred windows. But it was no use. On every occasion, the locks and bolts and doors were burst wide, leaving the diamond lying there, unprotected, for anyone, who wished, to handle.'

'Yet the stone itself was never touched?'

She shook her head. 'No. But it could have been. It was merely a matter of time, wouldn't you say? That was the frightening thing. As if whatever had been conjured up by the curse was laughing at them, playing with them. Waiting.'

'It sounds a bit . . . far-fetched,' demurred Bevan.

'One might say so,' smiled Theda, 'except that both my father and grand-father were there at the time. And that was what truthfully happened. The report of eye-witnesses.' She glanced up at him. 'You can't imagine Lawrence — even when a boy — being taken in by anything fraudulent, can you? He says it was quite uncanny. As if something invisible and malevolent had entered the room, twisting locks and bending bars . . . Bursting boxes, lifting latches, in a frenzy of destruction — The sheer power of the thing was breathtaking. One oak door was actually wrenched from its massive hinges . . . '

'Strange,' said Bevan.

'Devilish.'

12

'I don't like the idea; it's devil's work.' In
the Whites' outhouse, on the far side of
the Langdon estate, Seth faced his wife
across a bench littered with pieces of
touchwood. 'I don't like the idea,' he
repeated. 'It could be dangerous. Nerves
are too raw in the village for games like
this. You know how people behaved last
time; the whole witchcraft scene got out
of hand, with talk of Satan-worship in
every home . . . And it ended in tragedy.
Suppose you're caught?'

'I shan't be caught,' said Elise, folding a
dark cloak into a basket. At least, not
without deliberate intent, she wouldn't.
'And this is different. I'm not about to
start up a coven, or whatever. This is for
our own protection, my love. If our
movements were seen on the night we
reburied Amos — and obviously, if they
were, we weren't recognized — then a
couple of nights more of this kind of sick

activity will give people something more concrete to think about. Lay the dust and speculation about us and your father. And his grave. At least — ' she smiled thinly ' — everybody'll imagine the church and churchyard are again being used for Chatton Eastwood's former brand of dark purposes.'

'I hope you're right. But I still don't like it — ' Seth looked at her, troubled.

'Just stay here tonight, snug and warm, and give me an alibi, if I should need it.'

'I doubt if you'll convince the Reverend Oake that witchcraft's returned to his parish.'

'Oake will believe what he chooses to believe,' said Elise. There was a faint smile at the corners of her mouth. She lidded her basket, hiding the cloak with its fringings of touchwood, and stopped to place it on the floor beneath the bench, prior to following Seth through the inner door into the house. When she straightened, it was to find Cade Burrell at her elbow.

She moved sharply, but was too late to sweep the crumbled remains of the touchwood to the floor. It strewed the worktop from end to end, in broken, crusted pieces.

Cade traced his fingers through the debris.

'Getting ready for Hallowe'en?' he asked lightly. 'You're somewhat advanced.'

Elise laughed, brushing the fragments to the floor.

'It's good for kindling.'

'That's what I told the Reverend Oake, among other things.' Cade brought the sliver of touchwood Bevan had given him from his pocket and set it on the bench. 'There seems to be a deal of it around.'

Elise licked her lips. 'Oake gave you that?'

'Say, rather, that I purloined it. Removed the . . . um . . . evidence.' He grinned. 'Don't look so devastated. I'm not about to shop you. I thought you might like to know that Arthur Sullivan's been chin-wagging with the rector.'

'I thought he might.' Elise bit her lip.

Cade hunched a shoulder against the door-post.

'He says you witched his axe off its

handle and dropped it onto his shin.'

'If I'd done any witching,' said Elise bitterly, 'it would've landed in his skull. There's more than a few as'd be pleased to see the back of Arthur Stir-pot Sullivan.'

'You know what he's about, then? That he's saying the body found in the quarry was not Amos'?'

'Amos is dead,' said Elise flatly.

'I don't doubt it.' He gave her a speculative look. Whether Amos was or was not in the churchyard, he was dead. 'I was just warning you, that's all.' He smiled.

Elise eyed him squarely. Cade, she would trust with her life. Whatever he knew, or heard, or guessed, he would do nothing to harm her.

'Amos deserved anything he got,' she said.

'If we all got what we deserved, my dear, not many of us'd be riding white horses to the fair.'

'No.' She stared down, crumbling a piece of the touchwood between her fingers.

'It's none of my business,' he said gently, 'but if you're doing what I think you're doing — If you're hoping to deflect attention from . . . certain things . . . by substituting a little excitement of your own, then — '

'You're right, it *is* none of your business,' said Elise, green eyes suddenly cold. He had forfeited any claim to advise her, years ago.

'No . . . ' He sounded unsure. 'Still — take care.'

'Cade. We have our . . . reasons. You'll not split on us?' She indicated the spill of touchwood at her feet.

'You know me better than that.' He gazed down at the girl who had once seemed destined to be his wife, and whom his own nature had forced from him. 'But the rector might.'

She shot him a panicked glance. 'Mr Oake?'

'Arthur Sullivan went to him with a story about Amos having been dead long before that body, said to be his, was found in the quarry. Told him a rigmarole about you and Seth having conspired to cover up the real death because of foul play, and how you had then contrived to bury a tramp in Amos' so-named resting-place, to hoodwink everyone — Oake was rather perturbed about it all. He suspected Sullivan was trying some kind of shake-down, and he mentioned the tale to me, to see if I thought there could be any grain of substance in it.'

'And you said?'

Cade smiled. 'I told him the truth. That with Amos gone, Arthur Sullivan was the biggest rogue in Chatton Eastwood, and would sell his grannie for a clothes' — peg . . . '

Elise let out a faint hiss of relief. So far, then, so good.

'You don't think the rector's discussed Arthur's rotten lies with anyone else, do you?'

'No. It appeared to be very much against his principles to take me into his confidence,' returned Cade wryly. 'But he had to talk to someone. He regards me as his friend, and trusted me to keep my mouth shut. Poor sod.' He stepped through the doorway into the sunshine.

Turned. 'It's a breathing-space for you, Elise,' he said quietly. 'No more. The man's not a fool. He'll chew on every last little detail, and probably, eventually, when he recovers his second wind, he'll pump Arthur Sullivan dry. *If* there's anything to be found out . . . ' He left his sentence deliberately unfinished.

Elise lifted her shoulders in a graceful shrug. Raised tranquil eyes. There was more than one way of skinning a cat. As the Reverend Oake would soon find out.

She walked to the back gate with Cade, saw him off across the fields. Came back.

Seth was waiting for her, leaning on his arms across the sill of the open kitchen window.

'You heard all that?' Elise tilted her face to him.

He nodded. 'Enough, anyhow. What do we do now?' He gave a bitter smile. 'Take to the hills?'

Elise laughed. 'Oh, I don't think that will be necessary, my love.' Her green eyes mocked up at him. 'I come from a long line of witches, remember — '

The moon was up when Bevan

returned home from Langdons', taking his usual short cut through the church-yard. A cold, white moon in a vast, starry sky, lighting his way back to his cold, empty bed. He tripped clumsily on a tree-root. Steadied himself.

He had, he thought, drunk too much wine. Easy enough to do, in that company. Funny, the more light-headed, the more irresponsible, the more bearable life became. For a while, anyhow. Not that he still grieved painfully for Julie; at least, he didn't consider he did. In fact, sometimes he could hardly remember her face. Only her eyes. Greenish-gold and full of stars. And, recently, even those rose before him merely as part of another — living — face . . . But unwise to dwell on that . . .

Tonight they had discussed what they might conceivably be doing twenty years hence — a game, really, played over fine, old brandy. But one that had depressed Bevan utterly. Twenty years on? Where would he and Jonathan be? Rattling around still in some big, draughty house — together? Hating each other's guts, but politely pretending otherwise? Stabbing at each other with vicious, guilty barbs under the guise of brotherly affection? Or would the strained politeness have gone, leaving only the snarling pain? Hideous thought.

Bevan guided his wandering feet back on to the pebbled path.

Approaching the church, he recalled the shrouded figure of the previous night. It had been no child in that cloak and hood, he was sure. No man, either, if he were any judge. Some deluded female, then, set to call up Satan? His lips twisted wryly. He felt completely inadequate to deal with this, his flock's darker side.

However, it was his duty to check that all was well.

He headed purposefully towards the building. The moonlight struck the leaded windows in shining splinters, making it impossible to determine whether there was light within. Everything seemed quiet enough.

Pushing open the heavy west door, he peered through, his eyes flashing towards the altar at the far end.

Again, it was candlelit and, almost, he felt no surprise. Subconsciously he had been expecting something of the sort. Two candles, this time. Black. And burned away to thickish stubs. The air was heavy with their sweetish, drugging fragrance.

With slightly wavering feet he made his way forward to blow them out. The curls of grey smoke from the extinguished wicks rose up in his face to choke him. Swaying, he clung to the side of the altar, fighting a sudden bout of nausea. Then he turned, eyes ranging the length and breadth of the little stone church. Nothing to see. Nothing that was unusual or wrong or out of place. Rows of empty pews in the moonlight, the dark gape of the pulpit, a reflected pale shine from the white marble font . . .

He took a deep, steadying breath. Picked up the dead candles. Their stench was still overpowering, a decadent, ruttish smell reminding him of past intimacies and bodily warmth and bed. And the door was shut. Perhaps if he opened it, let in the fresh air —

He staggered rather than walked towards the door. Threw it wide.

The churchyard lay quiet in moonlight, its gravestones glistening, silent ghosts. Beyond, the surrounding yews were a wall of gloom.

Bevan drew the church door closed behind him, took deep breaths of the fragrant night-scented air. The action served only to set his senses reeling. In his half-dazed state he wasn't at first sure if he had really seen it, that flickering movement by one of the older gravestones beneath the trees, but a second survey convinced him. Someone was standing on top of the flat-topped stone. Someone — or something. Then it moved again, back into total shadow, and seemed immediately to take on an eerie luminosity of outline. He stiffened. No mistake now. A figure. *The* figure, cloaked and hooded in faint, trembling light. Bluish. Phosphorescent.

Without further hesitation, Bevan dashed forward, leaping grave-mounds in his stride.

But this time his quarry did not run.

It stood its ground, held wide its arms.

And the cloak fell clean away.

It was Elise. Bevan registered the fact too late as he flung himself on her, grabbing at her tumble of hair.

Elise, and naked as Eve.

Her body was a pale flame in the dimness.

He tried to gather his scattered wits, to turn; at least to pull away from her a little, but she was too quick for him. She was in his arms, pressed against him, thigh to thigh, and breast to breast; her lips on his, her hands about him, touching him, undoing him, caressing him in ways which he realized he had almost sponged from mind, and which called forth shudders from his all-too-willingly responsive flesh. And then she was drawing him forward into moonlight, forward and down, among the grassy hummocks of long forgotten graves . . .

Behind them, in darkness, Bevan could discern the heap of discarded cloak, a soft spectral outline which seemed to hold the fading luminescence of a thousand dying glow-worms. While, all around them, the sweet-sharp, pineapple smell of chamomile rose like water. Long afterwards, he would do penance for the ease of her seduction of him, but at the time it did not matter. The tumult in his body and brain obliterated all sense and reason; all honour. And perhaps he did not wish it, will it, to be otherwise —

Later, too, he thought she could have received little pleasure from him. It had been so long since he had had a woman, or even wanted one, that he was unable to hold himself in check, and it was swiftly over. But while it lasted, the entire world shrank to that one small patch of rough-grassed ground; to the arch of her body across the grave, the touch of her hands, the seeking, warmly desirous mouth, the wholly female, rounded softness and open invitation of her . . .

To the shock of ecstasy.

Then it was finished.

And she was gone.

He came to his senses alone, with the metallic taste of excitement still on his tongue; her perfume a lingering breath in his clothes, and a faint, betraying silvery trace of touchwood powdering his skin.

13

Following the rough footpath across the meadow which stretched behind the Jobbers' Arms, Arthur Sullivan rolled his drunken way homeward. Two days had passed since his fruitless meeting with Lance Langdon, but young Langdon had not been his only target that day and Arthur had subsequently talked himself into a windfall. He patted the bottle in his pocket. Plenty more where that had come from, he thought groggily, as he set his unsteady feet on the rickety plank bridge that crossed a little stream. Too small even to have a name, the water rose from a spring higher above the village, ran for countless yards beside the narrow road known appropriately enough as Watery Lane, and then dived beneath the hard surface to trickle a boggy, undulating track downwards through fields and woodland towards the river Chatton.

With a sharp turn to his left, Arthur

pursued the path beside the stream. Even in dry weather, the ground there was always moist and smelled strongly of dank vegetation and wet soil, and here and there the banks were heavily grown with alder. Although the trees were in full leaf and it was evening, daylight still flushed the sky with its long, lingering summer brightness, so that walking under the close green branches was no more alarming than entering into a lightly curtained room.

The man had had an uncomfortable skinful and his steps were rather less than sure; but there appeared little danger to his life or limbs on the pathway. If he slipped — and he slipped often, cursing loudly each time he did so — then he could do nothing worse than soak his trousers to the ankles.

Once, he stopped to relieve himself beside a patch of butterbur, whose great, rhubarb-like leaves, layer upon layer, spread out like crinolines. And once, startled into stillness, when some wild creature splashed noisily through the shallow water in front of him. Still standing, heart pounding painfully, he peered about him. Darker now, under the trees, the daylight almost fled, and all around him, the faint rustles and stirrings of the awakening nighttime world. The smell of damp leaves. Of water-mint. The clear, cool voice of the stream.

Nothing to fear.

Unbidden, the thought came: Amos White had felt as secure — in another place, on another day . . .

Arthur swallowed.

His eyes swivelled slowly from side to side. He forced his feet to move. Slipped. Caught at a branch of alder.

Take it easy, he told himself. Pulled the whisky-bottle from his pocket. Treated himself to a generous slug. And another.

A good pal, ol' Amos. Not right, what they said of him. Not right. Good . . . pal. He licked his lips. Had another pull at the whisky. Got it in for ol' Amos, the villagers had. Didn't understand, they didn't. Blamed him for . . . Blamed him . . .

Arthur blinked blearily.

No cause to blame his . . . pal. Not ol'

Amos. Not for . . . beating his children. No cause at all. Had to, didn't he? Didn't they see? Wicked . . . Wickedness . . .

Beat out the Devil.

That was right, wasn't it?

He took a tottering step forward, still clinging to the branch.

All lies, what they said. All lies. He knew. Amos had told him . . .

But Amos was gone. No more Amos . . . No more ol' pal . . . No more Elise, now, either . . . Elise — Gone. Everyone, gone. A slow tear trickled down his cheek.

Poor ol' Amos . . . Poor ol' Arthur.

Taking another unsteady step forward, he slipped, fell to his knees and remained there for a few seconds on the slimed ground, head bowed. Then, still clasping the whisky-bottle in one hand and stretching out to grip a convenient branch with the other, he struggled to rise. But he never made it. Too late, he heard the muted footfall behind him and half turned to see the upraised arms, the tightly clenched hands, bone-white around the lethal-looking piece of wood which swung towards him.

Stars exploded in his head and he went straight down, without a cry, to lie in a senseless heap on the muddy path.

For one moment, his assailant stood staring down at him. Then the hands dropped their weapon into the water and took hold of the fallen man by his collar, dragging him slowly and unceremoniously towards the stream and over the bank. His head and shoulders glissaded downwards. Water splashed on his forehead, on his hair, his eyes, his cheeks; ran in rivulets inside his collar, soaking his shirt.

The determined hands heaved him forward and left him there, his feet, legs, and hips on the bank; his shoulders and his head in the shallow, moving water; face down.

His assailant left him there. And walked away.

★ ★ ★

The death of Arthur Sullivan caused little except relieved ripples in the village of Chatton Eastwood, and more than one member of the community drew an easier breath at his sudden demise. Arthur, while drunk, had slipped and fallen into the stream and drowned himself, and good riddance was the general opinion.

Not one shared, however, by the police. An examination of the body left them far from convinced that the man's death had been purely accidental. There was, for example, the damage to the head. Possible, no doubt, for it to have been chance inflicted by a fall. The blow would have knocked the victim unconscious, and if he had also landed in the water . . .

No sign, though, of the object on which he had hit his head. Or which had hit him.

And there were those scuff marks along the ground. Had the body been dragged? Or had the man himself — possibly — recovered from the blow to his head and, half-dazed, hauled himself to the reviving stream, only to collapse again?

Yet, then, back to the missing rock, or brick, or branch, or whatever . . . Or weapon?

A detailed examination of the ground

yielded little. Footprints, a few. But most of the people nearby used the path at some time or another — or said they did. Slow, patient questioning of everyone in the locality was the order of the day.

Almost imperceptibly, the village closed its ranks.

If someone had murdered Arthur, then it was going to be difficult to prove. Without luck, the police would get nowhere.

Luck, and dogged patience.

But, somewhere behind all those shuttered faces, there hid the truth. Someone — maybe — had had sufficient reason to want Arthur Sullivan dead. And had acted.

Maybe.

The police carried on asking their questions.

★ ★ ★

'If they knew what cause I had,' said Seth bitterly, watching the two detectives making their departure through the cottage gate, 'I'd be their prime suspect.'

208

'Well, they don't know,' said Elise reasonably, 'so quit worrying.'

'But if they ever found out that Arthur was blackmailing us . . . over Amos — '

'That's highly unlikely. He didn't broadcast it.'

'One whiff of that and they won't just dig into things, they'll bloody well excavate,' said Seth desperately.

'They're not going to find out.'

'Cade Burrell knows, and the rector.' He flung her a worried glance. 'Cade won't tell the police anything, I'm sure, but I don't know about the Reverend Oake. He might feel it's his duty to say something.'

'Oake will keep his mouth shut,' said Elise firmly.

On two counts. One, he'd not want to harm her, he had enough warm feeling for her to protect her and her husband that far. No, he'd not pass on any slanderous rumour, for rumour was all it had been to him. And, secondly, he'd keep quiet, anyway, on his own account. If he shopped her, Elise, then he might very well believe that she would retaliate by telling the world of his seduction in the churchyard. Not something he'd want to live with, she'd surmise. Besides, any revelations of his about her and Seth would then smack of petty spite, and she doubted if the police would reckon the story enough to go to all the trouble of obtaining permission to dig up the graveyard. Not on such a shaky say-so.

'Did I know whether Sullivan had any enemies?' Seth's bitter voice broke into her reverie. 'He must have had, mustn't he, if they believe that somebody killed him? And I told them so. Almost everyone in Chatton Eastwood, at a rough guess. But I imagine I'm number one on their list. They knew all about that fight I'd had with the damned man. How he'd assaulted you . . .'

'The whole village knew about that; Arthur had the bruises,' replied Elise serenely. 'It means nothing, the police have said almost the same kind of thing to nearly everyone. You know you didn't kill Arthur — if anyone actually *did*. There has to be opportunity as well as motive, and you were safely tucked up in bed the night he died. We had an early night. Remember? I can confirm that. And so can Kathie, if she's pressed. Besides, as you've said, there were plenty of others with good enough reason to want him dead.' She turned to smile at her husband. 'So the police can go and bark up some other tree. Up Langdons', for example. Arthur told me that much himself. That the young Langdons had something to hide.' Her smile broadened and she leaned forward to kiss the side of his jaw. 'What do you think Lance has been up to?'

'Nothing that would warrant murder.'

'Arthur said, to ask him about Frognalls bridge. In April.'

Seth paled. 'Sullivan saw that?'

'Saw what?'

'Lance Langdon at the bridge. But, even so, it would hardly be a reason for murder.'

'What would hardly be a reason for murder?' Elise's voice was impatient.

'Langdon moved that child. Young Robin Goode. God knows why. I thought he was taking the boy to hospital, or something, although from the way the kid's head was lolling he looked a goner to me. Broken neck, I'd have said.'

'You saw it?'

Seth nodded miserably. 'Yes. I was up in a tree by the bridge. There's a group of ivy-covered oaks there — you know where I mean . . . ? Well, you can see for miles from up there. There's a marvellously clear view of the bridge, and of the river on either side, and of the road down the hill and where it curves to right and left past Frognalls estate — '

'Yes. I guess there would be. But what were you doing up a tree?'

He looked momentarily uncomfortable and, for a few seconds, his eyes slid away from hers. When they returned to stare straightly into her own they were very green and bright, and slightly defensive-looking.

'From there, one can also see right over the Frognalls' wall, into the actual estate. There's a man there — one of the estate workers — who knows me, and tosses over some game from time to time. The odd hare or pigeon; sometimes a pheasant or partridge or two . . . Things like that. Even an occasional crate of stuff from the house — '

'Stolen?' Elise's voice was sharp.

'No . . . I don't think so.'

'You'd better be more certain than that, my lad. Sounds pretty fishy to me. However, leaving that aside for the time being, go on, you were explaining about Lance Langdon . . . '

'I saw his Land-Rover parked on the other side of the bridge, among some bushes there; I doubt if it could have been seen from the road . . . And Langdon himself — '

'What was he doing?'

'He seemed to be checking the river depth, so far as I could tell. We'd had some rain, and a lot of melted snow, earlier, and the water-level was much higher than usual. Nothing to cause alarm, though.' He shot her an elliptical green glance. 'Then the boy came racing down the hill on his bicycle, and smack into the wall — You know, where Stevens got his bundle? Anyhow, I was going to climb down, to see if there was anything I could do — although I was sure it was all up with the kid, because he'd packed an almighty wallop with his head — when along comes Langdon, scrambling up the bank from the river. And he picks up the lad and puts him and his bicycle into the back of the Land-Rover. I thought he was rushing the child to a doctor, or to a hospital, but he must have unloaded him along the Hatchins road, and left him there. Made it look like a hit-and-run death. Easy enough to do, I imagine. The bicycle was a write-off. And the wall around Frognalls estate is built of the same stone as that which lines Hatchins ditch.'

'But why would Langdon do that?'

Seth shrugged.

Elise stared at him. 'It doesn't make sense. He didn't kill the child, so why should he want to cover up the death, or alter its place of origin in any way? The whole thing was an accident, pure and simple, so you say, without Lance being anywise involved — ' She paused. 'Unless he imagined that he might be blamed, somehow, for the boy's death. After all, he had no idea that you had seen what had happened; could clear his name.' Her gaze swept over Seth again. 'You're sure the Land-Rover was in no way mixed up with the accident?'

'Quite sure.'

'And you didn't mention the sorry affair to anyone?'

Seth shook his head. 'There was no point. Nothing could have been done to help the boy; he was dead. No one was being blamed for his death — only some faceless, nameless, hit-and-run merchant. It was best to leave things as they were. To have come forward and told the truth, to have said that he had been shifted by Langdon, might have upset the parents even more, brought them greater pain, and would certainly have made trouble for Langdon. And he wasn't a criminal. Not how I saw it. No. Best to say nothing — '

'It looks as if Lance might have had his own reasons for wanting the child away from there. Did you spot anything else? Anything which might have accounted for his odd behaviour?'

'No. There was nothing *to* spot. I saw the kid skeeter down the hill on his bike, skid and hit the wall by the bridge. Even from where I was, I could tell his neck had been broken. I was going down, but Langdon got there first, examined the boy, picked him up, loaded his bicycle after him and drove off. And that, I thought, was that. A nasty, fatal accident.'

'Only it turns out that the nasty, fatal accident happened in another place entirely.'

'Mmm.'

'Are you quite sure that Langdon had nothing to do with it? The boy didn't hit the Land-Rover, or swerve to avoid it, or anything? He wasn't startled by its horn?'

'No.'

'And you saw nobody else? Not Arthur Sullivan, for example — ?'

'No, and if he *was* there, then he would have had to have been flat in the ditch on the far side of the river.'

Elise moved restlessly. 'You should have said something.'

'Like what? That Langdon was lying? A nice load of unpleasantness that would have made . . . ' His expression darkened. 'And the police would have had to question me. Have you thought about that? I wasn't feeling so pure that — ' He bit back the rest of his sentence. Shot her a quick, slanting look.

'No.' She understood. So his reasons for being up that tree were not strictly legal; she'd guessed as much. She said, returning to her original theme: 'Arthur Sullivan had some kind of hold on a lot of people, and Arthur Sullivan was found dead. He hadn't been robbed; he was definitely drunk. He could have fallen, hit his head, rolled into the water — '

'Very likely.'

'On the other hand — '

'He could have been done in.'

'So. A list of those who wanted him out of the way. Lance Langdon, seemingly, for one . . . '

'I've told you, moving that child might have been foolish, but it could hardly have been grist for blackmail. And if Arthur did try it on, then that fact certainly wouldn't have merited his murder.'

'Well, perhaps we don't know the whole of it. Maybe it would pay us to take a closer look at that bridge — ' returned Elise smartly. 'Anyhow, if not Lance Langdon, there were plenty of others gunning for Arthur. Jim Burns, for example. He was after Sullivan's hide because the old goat'd been messing about with his daughter.'

'Again, hardly a sufficient motive for murder.'

'No, but you must admit, not many people liked him. He was always causing trouble in some form or another; telling tales; stirring things up.' She stared past him reflectively. 'Cade Burrell hated him. Did you know that? Sullivan set the village on him over young Michael.'

'That was ages ago.'

'Hurts can rankle.'

Seth grinned. 'And if it were Cade who'd nobbled Arthur, you'd not be likely to say so — not to the law.'

He walked with her across the grass.

'I would — to save you. Can you think of anyone else who might have had a good reason for wanting him dead?'

'Me,' said Seth.

Elise threw him a look of frustration.

'We've already ruled you out.'

'As far as I can see — and as far as the law would be concerned — if they ever found out about Amos, and about Arthur's blackmail, then my motive would loom very large.' His voice was dry. 'Two for the price of one.'

'Lucky you have an alibi for one of them, then,' said Elise sourly. 'And I wish you'd forget about Amos. He's in his grave.'

'So long as he stays there . . . ' Seth turned and, swinging his rabbit-catcher — the contraption the rector had once termed *bolas* — made his way through the back gate and across the field towards the wood.

14

Bevan Oake, watching from the hedge-row, waited until Seth had gone from sight before crossing the patch of open ground to Elise.

She saw him coming and stood quite still, her stance, and her expression, unwelcoming.

'I came — ' he began.

'I know why you came,' she said.

She hadn't expected him so soon. He must have spent but a brief period wrestling with his conscience, if he had one, she thought bitterly. But it was too dangerous to turn him away now. Suppose he said something to the police? She was almost sure he wouldn't, but still . . . Better to play along. One more twist to the knot. And on this occasion he had come to her . . . However, he must be made to understand that this would be the last time. The very last time. She'd have to point out the dangers, the

difficulties, appeal to his Puritan core
. . . Where was his moral fibre? . . . Her
lips twisted.

'Come inside,' she said.

'No,' he said quickly, panicked. 'No.
You misunderstand — '

'I do?' The eyes she turned on him
were full of mockery.

'Yes. I came — ' Why had he come? To
apologize. Or so he had believed. To beg
her pardon for — For what? For being
weak? For not having had the strength to
save her from herself? God. Even in his
own head it sounded feeble, priggish,
crude. Words of chaff from a man of
straw. And it was all untrue. Now he
stood there, he knew that. Knew his
subconscious had played him false. Part
of him had come to take up where he had
left off in the graveyard. The strongest
part? Even the sight of her made him
ache. To touch her —

'The . . . cherries . . . ' he said faintly.

'What else?' Again, an edge of mockery.
'Come inside.' The hand on his wrist was
cool.

Minutes later he was in the kitchen,

without any true understanding of how he had arrived there. His eyes took in the unwashed dishes, the bread still upon the table, the line of newly-ironed shirts hanging across the far end of the room beside the stairs, an open door to which they were heading. A tumbled bed.

A faint shudder went through him.

Elise felt the tremor and turned.

'Kathie's room,' she said practically. 'She's out. Will be for some time.'

She guided him in and closed the door, and his arms came up and round her. He lowered his head.

Lord have mercy upon us . . . The familiar chant in his skull, washed away on a rising tide . . .

Several geological ages later, he stood again beside the door, his fingers fumbling at his clothes. Nothing had changed. The sun had wheeled a little further, perhaps; the air become a fraction hotter, but the bees still hummed busily in the roses outside the window, and woodpigeons still purred.

But he knew he had held her for the last time. He had arrived to apologize, and had stayed to love, and he loved her still — but he would never touch her again. Not because he was strong, or repentant, or ashamed . . . He wasn't. He felt neither sorry for his actions, nor bowed with disgust. He knew that now. And if he remained in Chatton Eastwood he'd doubtless demonstrate that fact all too clearly — whenever she let him . . .

But she was married to Seth.

Not an insurmountable obstacle, surely, whispered a demon in Bevan's ear.

He smiled bleakly at her. For him, yes.

She didn't love him and, whatever her motives for allowing him to bed her, the sexual act itself was not enough and never would be.

Elise sat watching him from the pillows.

She saw his eyes range the disordered room, going from the small slippers kicked into one corner, to the heap of grubby clothes upon the floor; flicking from there to the tissues and talcum spilled on a table, making a quick, all-round inventory until they rested once more on the rumpled bed.

'Kathie's room?' His face wore an expression of distaste.

'More practical than a gravestone,' said Elise. Her green-gold eyes mocked up at him. 'And I'll not cuckold my husband in his own bed.'

Bevan opened the door and went out, and shut it behind him with a gentle, and very final, click.

★　★　★

Night came with welcome cloud and a spattering of warm rain against the window-panes. The day had grown increasingly airless and more sultry as it had progressed, and the evening had brought no relief. Merely a breathless, sticky humidity that hung over every-where like a pall. Thunder grumbled in the far distance.

Elise had gone to bed early, pleading a headache and fending off Seth, and had fallen almost immediately into a deep, dreamless sleep. She awoke to the whispering rain and to the noise of raised voices from the kitchen below.

Seth's side of the bed was still empty.

Swinging her legs to the floor, Elise padded to the door. Grabbed at a cotton robe there. Listened.

Seth. And Kathie.

The young girl's voice was high and hysterical. Full of tears. Seth sounded angry.

'It's your own damned fault,' he was saying. 'You could have — '

The rest of his sentence was cut off by his sister's rejoinder, unintelligible through its stormy rush of tears.

Elise sighed and started down the stairs.

Both combatants saw her at the same instant and froze, eyes wide, lips slightly parted.

A tableau of guilt, if ever there was one, thought Elise with an inward laugh. Partners in misdemeanour, if not in crime. Something to do with the ill-gotten gains from Frognalls, maybe?

She had barely reached the bottom tread when Kathie whirled about and ran for the outer door. Was through it and had banged it closed behind her before

Elise could catch another breath.

'Whew! What's the matter with her?'

'She's upset.'

'I can see that. Where has she gone?'

Seth shrugged. 'Heaven knows.'

'You can't just let her run off into the night like that. You'll have to go after her, bring her back — ' Elise was struggling into her shoes.

Seth stood looking down at her.

'Where do you think you're going?'

'To find her.'

'She'll not thank you for it.' Elise, he could have told her, had been a fair part of his sister's grief.

'I know that.' She shrugged herself into a coat.

'We'll sort things out when she comes back.'

'She may not come back.'

Seth looked as if he didn't much care, one way or the other.

'Seth,' she said, pleadingly, 'come on. She's not fit to be out there in her present state, alone.'

'It's raining.'

'So? All the more reason to get her

back quickly. Seth. Love. Your sister's already tried to commit suicide once. She's unbalanced. Not in her right mind at present. She's bordering on some kind of breakdown — Have you any idea where she might have gone?'

Seth shrugged again. 'Possibly to the watchtower.'

'The watchtower!'

'She always goes there when upset.'

'Then come on. My God, if she throws herself over the edge . . . '

Seth stared at her, stunned. It was obviously a possibility that had never occurred to him.

Elise was out into the night quicker than he was, labouring against the now driving rain. It was dark and she had forgotten to bring a torch.

Seth, she saw, behind her, had been more provident. The small light in his hand wavered towards her, lances of rain caught in its beam.

'You're crazy,' he said against her ear. 'You're still in your nightgear. Go back.'

'No.' She was running now, one hand catching at the long robe to hold it high, and he was forced to lope beside her to keep up with her.

'I'll find her, bring her back. Go home, love.'

Elise ignored his plea and Seth did not again attempt to dissuade her.

Along the track at a fast stumble; down the road, its too-long-dry surface wet and slimy from the rain; past the bridge, and the stream, raindrops like chess-pawns bobbing on its dark water; and then a quick, undignified scramble up the watchtower hill, the rain in their faces, as they were reduced to hands and knees because the grass proved too slippery to negotiate upright. And always the fear that they might be too late; that the hysterical girl might already have jumped . . .

Elise raised her eyes to the top of the tower, where broken black walls gnawed at the paler cloud.

'Can you see her' she gasped.

'Yes,' he said quietly. 'And she's not up there.' He indicated, with a shaking hand, the place where his sister stood at the edge of the drop, silhouetted against the sky. Her hair whipped like a banner behind her, soaked with rain.

'Kathie,' husked Elise.

The girl turned her face.

'Go back,' she spat, 'or I'll jump.' She made a sharp little twist.

'Kathie!' Elise's voice rose to a scream, was carried away on the wet, night air.

'Kathie, come away from the edge,' said Seth quietly, taking a small step forward.

'Stay away!'

He stopped at once and the hand he had been offering to her fell to his side. What to do now? They appeared to have reached an impasse.

The rain was easing, but still thick enough to be wetting, carrying on it the fresh smell of washed grass and a floating sweetness from honeysuckle. A fragrance so familiar, so normal, that he had breathed it a thousand times. Stood there, on that same spot, and breathed it in. This nightmare couldn't be real, couldn't be happening. He blinked the rain from his lashes. A short flurry of wind, chasing the breaking clouds, blew, in its passing, a snowstorm of petals from the elder trees which grew around the watchtower.

'Kathie. Please.' Elise held out a hand.

No response, but a faint backwards sway from the wraithlike figure.

Elise bit back a gasp.

'Listen, Kathie, whatever the problem, it's not worth dying for. Come back home, and we'll talk. Something can be worked out.'

The small head turned to her, half-blinded by the whipping hair.

Encouraged, Elise held out her hand again. Took a step forward.

Kathie moved sharply back until she was teetering on the very brink of the drop.

Her two companions held their breath, let it out in a slight sigh. The girl had steadied, was watching them.

'Kathie — ' Seth, this time, his voice low and coaxing.

Her dilated eyes swung to his, clung there.

'Why'd you bring her?' she demanded. 'We don't need her, we've never needed her. We were all right as we were . . .' The savage little voice filled the night.

'I needed her,' said Seth quietly. 'Now stop being foolish and come home.'

'We were fine till *she* came. *Whore!*' The final word spat towards Elise.

Elise flinched, but said nothing.

Seth said, still quiet: 'I love Elise. Nothing can alter that. No hysterics, no tantrums, no tears . . . But I love you, too, and nothing can change that, either. Elise would be fond of you, too, if you'd let her — So come home.'

'God damn Elise!' The curse took off into the night sky. 'You think she loves you? Then tell her the truth. See how much she loves you then. Let's stop living lies. Tell her when Amos really disappeared, when you really killed him. Tell her that. Let her work things out. And see if she still loves you . . . '

Elise felt the man beside her go stiff with shock. She turned to him but his face was a white blur in the dimness and she could not read it.

'Go on,' shrieked Kathie. 'Tell her!'

'What does she mean?' asked Elise softly. 'What is she talking about? What truth about Amos?'

Seth did not answer her. He still stood like a man in shock, unable either to move or speak. He couldn't believe that Kathie would do this to him. They had always hung together, no matter what. Cared and covered for each other.

'You think Amos walked out on us in April? Just before you slithered in?' Kathie had turned to Elise again. 'You poor fool. He was in his grave long before that. Ask Seth.'

Seth moved then. Moved and spoke. One word.

'Don't — ' he said.

His voice held pleading.

But Kathie was too far gone to heed him.

She took a short step towards them. 'Our father went missing during the first week in January. If Seth killed him, then he killed him then. More or less as soon as he could move after the beating Amos had given him.'

'January?' Elise's voice was bewildered. So, Seth had lied, tacked on a month or two; it hardly seemed to matter. January, or April, Amos was dead. It was several moments before she grasped the significance of the shift in time.

'The baby,' she whispered. 'It can't be Amos'.'

'Of course it's not Amos',' shrieked Kathie. 'Do you think I'd carry a child of his!' The tears poured down her cheeks. 'It's Seth's. Ask him.'

She made a frantic little move back towards the cliff's edge and both Elise and Seth instinctively flung themselves forward, grabbing at the swaying girl, and they all went down in a tangled heap on the wet grass.

'It's all right, Kathie; it's all right,' soothed Elise. 'Everything's all right.' Patently ignoring the fact that everything was very far from all right. She struggled to put her arms round the girl. But Kathie had stopped fighting to pull free and had collapsed against her, weeping. Great shudders shook her frame, but they were, Elise saw thankfully, caused by tears of relief, a release from intolerable tension, rather than by those terrifying gusts of her previous hysteria. Elise felt her own face wet, but whether from the soft, light rain or falling tears she was not sure. Seth, too, was shaking. His arms were around them both and she could feel the tremors running through him and, for a time, they huddled together like three terrified children in a storm, not certain what the heavens held in store for them.

At last, Elise said firmly: 'No one else must ever know about this. You understand that, Kathie? To everyone else the baby is Amos'. Not by a word or sign do you ever show otherwise.'

She felt the girl make a shuddering little gesture of distaste.

'Kathie. If you love your brother, you will do as I say. Better that the child is believed to be Amos'. Believe me.' All would be well, providing no one realized just when Amos had actually died. 'Listen, Kathie, for all concerned, that way is best.' She avoided looking at Seth. Not that she harboured much blame for him. She could guess what had happened — the sorely-savaged young grab consolation where they can — and one slip was not going to remove her love from him.

'The truth would make it hard for Seth,' she said gently. 'Amos has gone, and the world can't hurt him, but Seth is here. And we, too, are going to have a child — '

For the first time since Kathie's outburst she looked at her husband. He was watching her, very white and still. God, she thought, what a muddle, what a ghastly mess. But no point in shouting recriminations from the top of watchtower hill. She forced herself to smile at him.

'It was,' said Seth with difficulty, 'just the once.' Not an excuse, but explaining. 'The day . . . after I'd had you — ' And that only made it sound worse.

'Was it rape?'

'No,' he said, very low. That much she had to know.

Elise drew a shaky little breath. Maybe that was a blessing . . . Maybe not. After a fractional pause she managed to smile at him again, and then at Kathie, and reached out and grasped a hand of each.

'I think we should go home,' she said.

15

By the next morning the rain had cleared. Elise stood in the sunny kitchen and watched mist smoking away from the drying hedgerows. Would that their own troubles could wreathe away as easily. With Arthur Sullivan's death she had imagined that any danger to them must have receded. She had been wrong: Amos still mocked them from his grave.

Behind her, Seth and Kathie sat at the table, dark heads netted in sunshine. Seth looked sheepish; Kathie, sullen. Both were silent.

Elise sighed. How could she ever have believed that the girl would have contemplated keeping Amos's child? Ridiculous, now, in retrospect, to have allowed the idea houseroom. But there must be no speculation about the man's death. Nothing that would lead anyone to re-examine the facts. For all their sakes, that must remain so. As for Kathie

. . . She sighed again. They would have to talk. Baldly. She swung round to face the girl.

'However distasteful, you must still pretend that Amos raped you.'

'Amos did rape her.' Seth's voice, like the winter wind.

'So that part was the truth?'

Kathie nodded, swallowing sudden tears. 'Yes,' she agreed with obvious reluctance.

'And then?'

'Seth swore he'd kill him.' The long dark lashes swept up. 'But Amos almost finished him first: he thrashed Seth to a pulp . . . ' A brief, agonized silence, remembering. 'Anyway, when Seth recovered, he went out one night — in early January, that was — and our father never returned from the pub in Melhurst. I guessed — I knew — that he was dead. That Seth had kept his promise.'

'True?' Elise turned to Seth.

Seth nodded. 'I dragged Amos from Kathie and was beaten up by him,' he said simply. 'When I could move again, about a week later, I collected a pickaxe and shovel from Langdons' toolshed and dug a grave in Dreaden's Wood. I knew the path my father took through the wood, so I hid, waiting for him . . . Killed him and dragged him to the open grave. Buried him.'

'How did you kill him?'

Seth stared at Elise as if he did not understand her question.

'How?' she repeated impatiently. 'With the shovel? Or a rock? . . . A blow to the head? . . . How?'

'I knifed him,' he said. 'In the back. I had to stab him several times; it was the only way. He was much stronger than I was . . . I told you.'

'You told me a lot of things,' said Elise bleakly. 'Some of them untrue. This time I want to be sure that I have all the facts right.'

He shot her a quick upward glance from under his lashes.

'It was your own fault,' he said quietly. 'You jumped to conclusions. In the beginning . . . When I said I'd killed my father you automatically assumed that I'd done it in April. After that — '

After that, it had been more politic to keep quiet. Or lie.

'Go on,' gritted Elise.

'That's all. I returned the tools to their racks at Langdons', cleaned myself up in the sink in their potting-shed — in case Kathie was awake when I got back: I didn't want to frighten her into fits — and then I came home.'

'Simple,' said Elise with bitter sarcasm.

Seth agreed bleakly. 'It was quite easy to hide the fact that Amos was missing from the rest of the village; the weather was bad, thick snow, freezing conditions, and our cottage is off the beaten track. No one came to see us and we went to see no one. Amos had been banned from the Jobbers' Arms, so nobody remarked on his absence there, and he hadn't been long enough a regular at the Cow in Melhurst for him to have established any kind of routine . . . '

'But how did you live?' Elise was puzzled.

'We managed.'

Elise stared at him. No money, no job, no handouts, equalled no food.

Kathie said: 'Seth is good at hunting. And a man over in Frognalls gave us things . . . Besides — ' She shrugged thin shoulders.

'Besides — ?' prompted Elise.

'There's plenty of stuff to be got round about, without anyone catching on.'

'Ah,' said Elise. 'I see.' The witchcraft caper. Or some of it, anyhow. A missing chicken here and there, the wide-open door, and the empty larder . . . Broken locks and stolen candles and disappearing wine . . . Seth had put his peculiar skills to effective use. And with enough astuteness to leave trademarks that would be readily recognized.

Seth said: 'We knew we couldn't go on like that indefinitely; sooner or later people would have to know that Amos had gone. But the longer the time that elapsed between his real and his supposed walk-out, the better. Or so I thought. If anyone became suspicious later on, surely the trail would be cold? . . . Langdons' burglary gave us an excuse to tell everyone that he was missing. People might not believe that Amos had engineered that theft, but they might at least consider he'd be capable of being in on the act; had collected his share of the proceeds, and skedaddled — he'd done it before . . . A further breathing-space for us, anyhow.'

'And then I arrived,' said Elise colourlessly.

He threw her another upward glance.

'Are you wishing you hadn't?'

'No.' That, at least, was true. And she'd fight tooth and nail for him, and for their happiness. Even so, it was days before she again remembered Lance Langdon's strange behaviour at Frognalls bridge, and recalled that Lance, too, had something to hide.

★   ★   ★

'Is this the place where Robin Goode skidded?' Elise stood in the centre of the bridge, opposite the Frognalls estate, and let her eyes roam the stretch of road before and behind her. It was mid July and, because it was also the day of the school fête, they would almost certainly have the river area to themselves.

Seth nodded. 'Just about where you're standing.'

'And the child hit his head — where?'

Slowly, Seth walked the length of the bridge and, crossing to the high, grey stone wall in front of him, indicated a section of the masonry. Sun and wind and rain had done their work, scouring the stones clean of any evidence that might once have been there.

'Where had Langdon parked his Land-Rover?'

Seth led her back across the road and a short distance along the bank of the river. Beside a sizeable clump of bushes — faded hawthorn and elder, twined through with long trails of greenish-headed wild clematis — he stopped and pointed.

'There,' he said. 'Less cover, then, though. April.'

Elise examined the terrain carefully; crouched among the bushes and cast her glance back towards the Frognalls' wall.

'You can't see the spot where Robin hit the stonework from here. You can't see the hill, or the bridge, either.'

Seth shrugged. 'Lance wasn't in the Land-Rover at the time, anyway. I told you. He was down by the river, near the pilings.'

'In the water?'

'That's right.'

Elise's brows knitted in a frown. 'What would he be doing in the water?'

'I don't know.' Seth stared at her. 'He was wearing waders. I thought he was checking the water-level against the bridge. That's where he was, underneath the outlet of that big drainage pipe — '

His finger pointed.

'That's not a drainage pipe,' replied Elise, pensively, her eyes studying the brickwork. 'It has nothing to do with the rainwater overflow. At least — ' Her gaze rose upwards. 'No. There you are. The drainage outlets are up there, much higher, closer to where the road runs . . . and much smaller — '

'So. What's that dirty great pipe for, then? Mansized rats?'

'Frognalls is a pierced bridge, built before the river level fell so drastically.

That pipe was intended to break the force of any flood water that came pounding at the structure. Or so Cade told me. In later years, I believe, piercing was incorporated in many bridges to make lighter constructions, with wider spans, but here it was used purely as a precautionary measure. Cade said it was never needed. Soon after the bridge was completed, the river shrank to its present piffling size and then dangerous torrents ceased to be a problem.' She altered her position on the bank so that she could obtain a better view of the large pipe-mouth.

'It's been blocked up,' she said.

'Uh?' Seth came to stand beside her. 'So it has. It's not noticeable unless you get level with it.'

'And, normally, no one would bother,' replied Elise thoughtfully.

'No. Too busy negotiating that sharp bend in the road.' Seth scowled. Walked to the far side of the bridge, and came back.

'The twin outlet on the other side is clear enough,' he said. 'Maybe this blockage was what Lance was investigating. Perhaps the pipe's silted up with rubbish, or something.'

'Hold on.' Elise had stooped and unbuckled her sandals, was kicking them off.

'What do you think you're doing?'

'Going paddling.' She grinned up at him and, before he could stop her, she was down the bank and ankle-deep in the clear, moving body of the river Chatton. A few strides brought her level with one of the cutwaters, those wedge-shaped bolsters which reinforced the base of the bridge and also served to cut, or lessen, the force of the water. They, too, were now no longer necessary.

Another moment, and she was climbing; stepping sure-footedly from one projection to another until she could balance on the topmost section of the cutwater.

Seth waded through the shallows to join her.

'Watch yourself,' he gritted. 'Check where you're putting your big feet.'

'It's perfectly safe.'

'Room enough up there for me?'

'Bags,' she said. She leaned forward and held out her hand. 'Come along up.'

She had, thought Seth, arriving beside her, exaggerated a little. There was room for him to stand locked to her armpit — just.

Her jet bracelet jangling against the brickwork, Elise was already exploring the orifice above her head with deft fingers.

'There's something jammed inside. Wrapped in plastic, I think, from the texture of it.' She juggled for several seconds with whatever lay under her hands. 'It's sliding forward . . . I felt it move. Heavy, though Not just a small package, I'd say. Big.'

'Here, let me try.' Seth raised his arms and locked his grip on the object which was now protruding a few inches from the mouth of the pipe. With spasmodic heaves he urged the bundle towards him and, slowly, it took shape. Cylindrical, solid, gleaming a dull silver through its transparent plastic, and looking, as far as they could judge, like some gigantic, silver-hued cigarette.

'What is it?' whispered Elise. 'A big gun? Some kind of cannon?'

'I shouldn't . . . think so,' replied Seth, gasping from his exertions. 'We'll find out in a minute.' He glanced sideways at her and grinned. 'You know, we're probably not supposed to be doing this. The thing's no doubt been put in there for a vital purpose — '

'Like what?'

'Well, to keep vermin out, or something. Stop birds nesting . . . ' He slid the cylinder-shape forward onto one shoulder.

'Birds and vermin have had free rein in there for centuries,' objected Elise. 'Why stop them now?'

'No idea. It was just a suggestion . . . ' He turned his head. 'Love, climb down into the water and steady this thing as I slide it forward and down towards you. There seems still more of it to come.'

'Looks like somebody's old, gift-wrapped carpet,' said Elise judicially, doing as she had been requested.

The object looked even more like somebody's rolled up carpet when it had been manhandled across the river, dragged to rest upon the bank and opened up. The plastic off, the cylinder had been found to be further securely encased in tinfoil and then in soft cloth.

'I know what is is,' said Elise in a small voice, as the final inner bindings were pulled away. 'Don't you?'

'Yes.' Seth's answer sounded equally strangled. He gave a jerk with his hands and the carefully-wound roll rippled away from him, uncoiling as it went. A thin muslin interlay lifted and drifted away like a wisp of cloud on some unfelt whisper of breeze. 'These are the missing Langdon tapestries.'

Both of them.

Spreading the articles gingerly on the river bank, Elise gazed down at the scenes before her. There was no mistake. She'd seen them often enough. Soft, rich silks that portrayed two renowned incidents from the Old Testament. Rude, Mrs Burrell had once said. They were, at least, instantly recognizable. Theda had told her that experts considered them to be unusual; wallhangings that were, strictly speaking, bastard creations, neither tapestry nor embroidery, but a rare combination of both, where the basic designs had been quilted and over-stitched as well as traditionally woven; a raised patch of blue flowers here, a plump-winged bird there . . . It gave a pleasing, three-dimensional effect to the whole, rather like later stumpwork embroideries. And added considerably to the value, Theda laughingly had said. Complementary, the pair of hangings together were worth a small fortune. Fragile, though. Not exactly mediaeval, as the village was wont to tell it, but near enough. Sixteenth-century, if she remembered correctly. And not to be mishandled as they had been. They had, Elise noticed, at some time been tacked to strong fabric, but presumably long before their present adventures.

The scene on her left, depicting a maniacal-eyed old man about to disembowel a bound, well-grown youth draped only in a gauze bandage which trailed inconsequently across his thighs, was, she knew, The Sacrifice of Isaac. The ram was hiding in a padded thicket. The other, far prettier in Elise's estimation, showed The Expulsion from Eden. Here, a scowling angel had, she supposed, already exiled the delinquent duo, whose sturdy bare legs were thrusting knee-deep through improbable flowers. A heavily-pregnant Eve, eyes coyly downcast, had one hand resting in a proprietorial manner on her husband's — reluctant — arm, the other curved beneath her swollen belly.

Was that, wondered Seth, also gazing down, an inherent pose of pregnant women? He'd seen Elise with her hand placed in just such fashion. Guarding? Protecting? Reassuring the life within? He glanced at his wife. No one could tell, by looking at her, that she carried his child. She appeared almost unchanged. Her waistline a shade thicker, maybe; her breasts a trifle fuller — Nothing that anyone would notice.

He watched her busy hands, skilfully and swiftly rewrapping the precious package.

'What are you going to do?'

She flicked an upward smile at him.

'Put it back. For the time being, anyhow. Until we know what happened, and why it was there.'

'Obvious, I'd say,' countered Seth. 'The bundle must have been hidden there after the robbery.'

'Yes,' agreed Elise. 'But it seems to have been very carefully done. Not something dreamed up on the spur of the moment, I'd guess. Why hasn't it been picked up? Removed? . . . And then there was Lance. Did he know it was there, do you think, or had he just spotted it when that child steamed down the hill?'

'Then forgot about it, later?'

'Easy enough to do, if he imagined it was merely rubbish; some alien object that was blocking the hole. Something kids had stuffed in there, perhaps. Not terribly important.' She stared across at him. 'The only alternative is to believe he *knew* the tapestries were in that pipe.'

'That he put them there himself, you mean?'

Elise nodded.

'But that makes no sense. Why should he? They were his. He could have sold them any time he chose. Unless . . . What about insurance?'

'No. Theda told me there was none. Too expensive.'

'So. What are we going to do?'

'Have a quiet word with Lance, I'd suggest. Whichever way you look at it, it's still his property.'

'His old man's, you mean. Technically.'

'Same difference.'

'I suppose you're right. Where to, now, then? Langdon House?'

'No. All the Langdons will be at the fête; Theda and Lance are presenting the prizes for the children's races . . . '

16

Chatton Eastwood's tiny primary school was bright with the flutter of bunting, and the sunny day had brought out the patrons in droves. Everywhere, including the tea-and-ice-cream vending stand in the school building itself, appeared to be doing a roaring trade.

Stalls of the more sedate kind had been arranged around the handkerchief-sized playground, and those of a more robust nature — bowling for the pig, coconut-shies, Aunt Sally, and the like — had been allowed to spill over on to the Village Green outside. At the far end of the Green, near the duckpond, and out of range of any stray missile, someone had considerately pushed — and abandoned — Jonathan Oake.

He stared around him morosely. It was not beyond his capabilities to take himself elsewhere, but there was nowhere else he wished to go. Not at this fête, anyhow. He wheeled himself under a tree and scowled discontentedly at the duck-fouled water. Damned village junkets!

A filthy, sand-stained hand thrust a polystyrene beaker full of tea towards him. At least, he presumed it to be tea: it was of a similar shade and consistency.

'Gran says, I'm to ask you if you want a bun.' The voice dared him to require any such thing.

Jonathan raised his eyes to his ministering angel.

Sally Pawcett. Built like a hatpin and with a mop of floss-white hair. She had a baby perched precariously on one skinny hip, and a band of hot and grizzling small children in rebellious tow. A large shoulder-bag was slung around her neck, bearing her down.

'I can live without a bun,' he said sourly. 'I can live without this muck, too.' With a twist of his wrist he upended the indeterminate liquid onto the grass. 'I don't take milk.'

'That figures. It'd curdle on impact.'

'Ah, a wit!'

'And the stuff's in an urn — you have it

254

as it comes,' she snarled, glowering at him from translucent eyes. 'It took me ages to ferry that tea across to you,' she went on, in justifiable fury. 'William spilled the first lot and I had to go back for another.'

'Nobody asked you to.'

'Gran did. And when Gran says jump, we jump.' The harsh little voice spoke with feeling. 'No joke, either, juggling William, the toddlers, this bag and that bally beaker, I might tell you.' She hitched the youngest child higher on her hip. It squirmed and, for one horrifying moment, Jonathan thought she was going to dump it on his knee.

'Get that goddamned kid away from me.'

'I'm trying to, aren't I? He's heavy, and he keeps slipping.' She scowled down at the man in the wheelchair. 'Rector's kin should be kind to kids.'

'It smells like a skunk.'

'He needs his nappy changing.'

'Well, you can't do that here.'

'Who said I was going to, Mister?' She glared at him through her fringe of white eyelashes. He'd seen poorer ones on a pig, thought Jonathan. Her eyes, too, were odd; so pale as to be almost without colour.

'You're keen on children?' He indicated the snivelling tribe with distaste.

'No, I'm not. And, what's more, when I get shut of this bunch I never want to see any of them again,' said Sally emphatically. 'I'll make darned sure I never have a kid of my own — '

'What about the joys of motherhood?'

'Joys!' responded Sally with bitterness. 'What joys? That starry-eyed crap must've been said by someone who didn't have any of the little perishers.'

'Or who had a nanny to look after them.'

'What's that got to do with anything?'

He grimaced. 'Nanny, as in nursemaid.'

'Huh!' The girl put out a grudging, conciliatory feeler. 'I could get you an ice-cream, if you like.'

'Don't trouble.'

'It's no trouble, or I wouldn't offer to do it,' retorted Sally. 'I'd like one myself and, if I say I'm taking one to you — poor soul — they'll let me have mine free.'

In spite of his annoyance Jonathan's lips quirked.

'Are you always so devastatingly honest?'

'Always,' she replied, with truth.

'Okay. Go ahead. Bring me an ice. And don't sample it on the way back.'

'Drop dead,' said Sally, from under a scowling brow.

When she returned, she was minus the gang of infants, although still strung about with the cumbersome shoulder-bag, and they licked their ice-cream cones for minutes in silence. Vanilla. Jonathan smiled inwardly. Vinegar might have been more appropriate.

'Where's the brood?'

'Elise — Walters, as was — has taken over for me. The mothers are supposed to collect their offspring before five, but they never do.'

'Couldn't you have got rid of that wretched holdall as well?'

Sally shook her head. 'It's full of gear to be taken to Langdon House after the fête. I've been detailed.'

'You've done your share, girl. Find someone else to deliver the goods.'

'Like who?'

'There's Cliff Burns over there, on his bicycle. Ask him to run the stuff along for you.'

She gave a crack of laughter. 'He'd never.'

'Yes, he will. If I say so.'

'Go on, then, ask him. But he won't do it; not even for you.'

She watched, amused, as he beckoned the boy over.

Cliff Burns came warily.

With a smile that more nearly approached a leer, Jonathan pulled a five-pound bank-note from his pocket. Flourished it in front of the startled youngster.

'Can you spare a few minutes of your valuable time to take this bag to Langdon House?'

'Right now?'

'Any time this evening will do, I guess.'

'Okay. Sure.'

Cliff made a grab at the bank-note, then, more leisurely, took hold of the object for which he'd accepted the bribe. He turned.

'There you are,' said Jonathan, as he

and Sally watched the boy depart with the bag, its straps now shortened, swinging from his handlebars.

'You offered him five pounds,' said Sally, in indignation. 'I'd have done it for five pounds . . . ' She scowled after the boy's retreating back. 'Cliff Burns'd do anything for money.'

'Most people will.'

'He'll probably forget to deliver the bag.'

'Undoubtedly, till he's good and ready. But he'll come through in the end. You see, it'll occur to him that there might be more pickings where those came from — if he's reliable.' He flicked a slight smile at the girl at his side. 'What dumb cluck suggested putting you in charge of the crèche?'

' . . . *And* the children's sandpit,' growled Sally.

'The crèche *and* the children's sandpit, then?'

'The rotten Reverend Oake.'

'My brother?'

'The same. Had a word in my Gran's ear, didn't he?'

Jonathan hid a smile.

The aggrieved voice went on: 'Thought it would be good for me! ... A dead giveaway, that. It was bound to be something I'd hate intensely.'

'That's life.'

'I haven't noticed the rector making any praiseworthy contribution to this afternoon. Where is he?'

'He's away. Gone into Retreat.'

'Gawd!' She flashed Jonathan a look from under the white lashes. 'Gran says he's had a nervous breakdown.'

'Then Gran's wrong, isn't she?' His eyes gleamed with amusement. 'Has she any more gems on the subject?'

'She believes Elise is trying to get her hooks in him.'

'Dear, dear. Do you?'

Sally shrugged. 'I think, if it were true, he'd be a fool to kick and squeal.'

'Not a strictly moral opinion, my child. That's her husband over there.' He nodded to another tree nearby, under which Seth White lay sprawled on the grass. He had his eyes shut.

'I don't like him.' Sally jerked her head

towards Seth. 'He's creepy.'

'You don't like anyone very much, do you?'

'That makes two of us.'

'I take it you don't like me?'

'Oh,' she said flippantly, 'for you, we have to make allowances — '

'Because I'm in a wheelchair? Don't let that bother you,' he returned dryly.

'It doesn't. I meant because you have to live with the pious parson.'

He flung her a startled glance. 'Oh?'

'Sanctimonious twit. A bit of real sinning might do him a power of good; make him more bearable.'

'I think he manages well enough in that direction,' grinned Jonathan, staring in a goading fashion towards Seth. Seth's eyes had flicked open and he was staring murderously back.

'He's glaring at you,' remarked Sally. 'In fact, he keeps glaring at you. What *have* you said to him?'

'This and that in passing,' murmured Jonathan. 'When he and his wife first arrived, about an hour ago.' He grinned. 'I think he took exception to some of my playful remarks about churchyards . . . and Elise being gravely overworked by my brother.'

'You were rude?'

'Oh, I expect so.'

'The rector trying to reform Elise, then?'

'I doubt it,' said Jonathan with a smirk, his eyes still on Seth, and aware that the younger man could hear every word he uttered. 'I'd say the boot was on the other foot entirely.'

'His holier-than-thou sermons make me sick. Do this, do that; don't do this, don't do that . . . Yuck!'

'I think that's the way of sermons,' smiled Jonathan, warming to her. She was that rarest of souls, a brutal critic of Bevan's. Most people acted as if his brother were first cousin to the archangel Gabriel.

''Guide us into the paths of peace'.' The girl mimicked Bevan's precise tones cruelly. 'I'd like to see anyone guiding Chatton Eastwood. All here've been at daggers drawn since the ark grounded.'

'I wonder there are any of you left.'

'Oh, we're thinning out,' said Sally in a flippant tone.

'What do you do when you're not squabbling with someone?'

'Pick my teeth,' she returned smartly. 'Or wash my hair.'

'Well, we all have our crosses to bear.'

She eyed him with dislike. 'Thanks.'

'Any time.' Jonathan appraised her, smiling. She reminded him of a dandelion-puff — the too long, thin body and that striking aureole of lint-white hair. She possessed no beauty now, but she'd age well. By the time she was sixty she'd look arresting rather than queer, he thought. Even now, in spite of its oddities, it was a compelling face.

The harsh voice recalled him to the present.

'What you staring at?'

You, my dear. You. But he was not mad enough to say it aloud. She had a tongue as sharp as her pointed little shoulder-blades and as cutting and mordant as his own. By sheer good luck he'd found her, this salty little person, and with her, his own salvation. And they would rub along

263

together very well. But it could wait. For a while.

'How old are you? Fifteen?'

'Mind your own business.'

'I'm aiming to make it my business,' he said — but only beneath his breath.

'I must go. I can see Elise waving.' She hesitated. 'Will you be all right here on your own?'

'Why? You fixing to find someone to hold my hand?'

She turned and, without another word, walked away from him.

★   ★   ★

No sooner was she beyond easy call, than Jonathan felt himself gliding inexplicably forward. He clapped his right hand to the brake. Somehow, the device had worked loose and the chair was rolling, of its own volition, down the short grassy slope towards the duckpond. With a hurried wrench, Jonathan snapped the brake sharply back into position. The chair halted. But no sooner had he taken his hand from the lever again, than it shot forward, releasing the locking bars on the wheels, and the chair ran forward again, smartly, almost to the very edge of the pond. Jonathan heaved the brake handle back and clung to it. Something must have gone wrong with the damned mechanism, he thought, frowning. It seemed incapable of locking the wheels. Even now, he could feel the bar fighting against his hand. What a cussedly stupid thing to happen, here, in front of all these people. And if he wasn't careful he was going to get a ducking. He tried, experimentally, to roll himself backwards, but the moment he eased his grip on the brake ready to turn the wheels, the chair began its former forward glide. Damn! He'd have to swallow pride and ask for assistance. A quick glance round soon convinced him that there was no one near enough to whom to explain his predicament. Even Seth had risen from his patch of grass under the tree and taken himself off to the pig-bowling stand. He was now leaning nonchalantly against the wooden hoarding, still staring in the direction of the wheelchair.

Double damn! thought Jonathan. He would have to shout to attract attention, summon help. But all his prideful inmost being cringed at the idea. No, better surely to wait? Sooner or later someone would be bound to come. Doggedly, he clung to the brake handle ... slowly jiggled himself around until he was sideways on to the water. He felt a little safer.

Just as he was congratulating himself on his manoeuvre, the chair sagged abruptly to starboard, taking on a frightening list. Jonathan tried desperately to cling to his seat, realizing that the whole framework was buckling beneath him. Too late, he cried out.

Suddenly, there were screams and shouts and the sound of pounding feet as people, alerted at last to his plight, came rushing to his aid.

Sally Pawcett turned, halfway across the Green, and, seeing what was happening began to retrace her steps at a gallop. Elise passed her, running at a tangent across her path. Not in the direction of the pond, however, but somewhere out to the far right. And she, too, was screeching.

'No, Seth, no!' she was crying. 'Stop it!'

Puzzled, Sally swung and watched her go, then as abruptly dismissed her from mind; Elise's actions could have nothing to do with the present accident. Seth White had been nowhere near Jonathan when it had happened, and nowhere near the pond. Was nowhere near there now. With a mental shrug, she carried on, swift-footedly, towards her former goal.

Elise reached Seth's side, panting.

'Stop it, Seth! Stop it!' she shrieked, thumping him with a flailing fist. He looked at her with vast, unseeing eyes. There was sweat on his upper lip.

Elise flung a frantic glance across to the pond. The fastest of the running, would-be rescuers was almost there, but, even as she watched, the wheels on the far side of the invalid chair crumpled like cardboard with a quite audible scrunch, and the helpless man was pitched into the water. The concertinaed chair tilted over and subsided languidly on top of him.

'Seth!'

He came back to her slowly, his eyes gradually losing their foggy glaze of concentration and becoming once more their usual brilliant, now smiling, greyish-green.

Elise flung another apprehensive look behind her. All right now. The rescuers had arrived, were doing their job, and Jonathan had not been in the water long enough to come to harm.

With a slight shudder of relief, she took her husband by the arm and led him unhurriedly across the grass towards the school. Once through the gates, they sat side by side on the wall of the deserted sandpit.

'Why did you do it?'

'Do what?'

'Come off it! You know what I mean.' She was breathing hard. 'It was a despicable thing to do to a handicapped man.'

Seth smiled at her and touched her lips gently with his fingers.

Elise caught at his hand. 'Don't ever do anything like that again. You might kill someone.'

He said lightly: 'People must learn to leave my family alone. 'I'll not have anyone speaking ill of you — or Kathie.'

'Seth! I mean it. Quit!'

'I love you.' He grinned. Wrote the words in the sand, running the symbols affectionately together. *SethandElise. SandE.* The best thing that had ever happened to him, Elise. And nobody, but *nobody*, was going to slight her name. His hand swept down, erasing her initial. *Sand.* Life was like sand. Shifting. Sliding through one's fingers. He was still staring thoughtfully down at his handiwork, when Elise spotted a familiar figure striding towards a parked Land-Rover.

'There's Lance Langdon. I've been waiting to catch him alone all afternoon. You coming?'

Seth pulled a face. 'No. You go ahead. You're better at that sort of thing than I am. I'm sure you'll call him a thief with the utmost diplomacy.'

'One can't thieve one's own belongings; and we don't know for sure that he was the one who lifted those tapestries, anyway.'

'No.' Seth smiled at her. 'Go to it, then. I'll see you at home; he's bound to offer you a lift.' He rose and, with a wave of his hand, went at a slow lope across the playground.

Elise made her way to the Land-Rover. 'Lance?'

The fair-haired man bending over the vehicle swung to her with a smile.

'Hello, Elise. You've survived the hectic afternoon, then? I'm just about dead on my feet, and if I have another mug of that revolting tea I'll throw up. Did you require a lift home?'

'A word with you, rather.'

'A dozen, my sweet — '

She told him, succinctly, of their find, while the smile on his face narrowed little by little until it faded away altogether.

'Our tapestries, you say? You're sure? Did you actually get a good look at them?'

'Yes,' said Elise impatiently. 'They are definitely yours. I'd recognize them anywhere.'

'Yes,' he said slowly. 'I imagine you

would.' He gripped her arm. 'Get in.'

'You're going there now? To Frognalls bridge?' She slid into the passenger seat of the Land-Rover. 'Where's Theda?'

'Probably already at the house.'

Elise was quiet beside him, until they turned sharply off the lane down which they had been heading and careened along the back driveway that led to Langdon House.

'You wish to collect your sister?' she asked him, briefly puzzled.

Lance did not answer, but ran the vehicle on to the grass at one side of the drive and stopped. Leaning backwards, he scooped up his shotgun from behind him.

'Get out,' he said.

'Here?'

'I said, get out.' His tone was full of frost.

Elise did as she was told, reluctantly. They were about halfway along the rear drive — which was rarely used and bore the cracked surface and unchecked spread of weeds to show it — and immediately opposite the old potting-shed.

Lance put a hand on her arm and propelled her roughly across the grass towards the ramshackle building. In his other fist he carried the shotgun.

17

The door sported a brand new, shiny brass padlock, but it was undone, swinging impotently from its hasp. Lance hooked it to one side, kicked open the door and gave Elise a violent shove.

'Inside!'

She had no choice but to obey.

Recovering her balance, she rounded furiously to face him, but he had already closed the door and was standing with his back to it, his shotgun cradled in his arms.

'What do you intend to do?' she spat. 'Shoot me?' She didn't really see how he could. Too noisy, for one thing. Too messy.

'Shut up,' he gritted, 'and sit down.' He nodded to a wooden chair behind her.

'And if I don't?'

'I'll break your arm.'

A sharp movement with the gun convinced her.

Elise sat. Gingerly, at first, perching on the edge of the old kitchen chair. A vicious prod from the gun-butt sent her hard back against the wooden rails.

'Put your hands behind you.'

Again, a command, and she did as she was told.

She stared up at him. 'Are you mad? . . . Seth will come looking for me.'

'Will he, indeed? But not for a very long time, I would imagine — ' Lance jerked her wrists together through the slats of the chair-back and, with a twist or two from a bundle of garden twine by his elbow, immobilized her hands. He grinned nastily. 'Or do you think I should go in search of Seth? Put him out of action, too? It might be a good idea.'

She was silent.

Lance tightened a knot. 'No? . . . And of course you're right. Waste of energy, I'd say. Seth will remain cosily in his cottage till bedtime. After that, he's welcome to come looking for you any time he chooses.'

'You'll not hurt him?' she begged.

'Hurt him? Now whatever makes you

think that I'd hurt him?' he mocked. His eyes flashed blue malice. 'Oh, I see. You're afraid he might have an unexpected accident — like Arthur Sullivan.'

He heard her breath go in on a gasp.

'Are you implying that you killed Sullivan?' Elise's voice was an incredulous whisper.

'Of course not,' he said contemptuously. 'I don't kill drunken old men, or even stupid boys and girls who poke their noses into places where they shouldn't . . . But that's not to say I wouldn't break a bone or two if I had to — So, watch it!'

'It *was* you who took the tapestries, then. Seth and I suspected as much when we found them.'

'Rather an obvious conclusion by now, I should imagine,' he said, the tightness of his face easing into a thin smile. 'And I've not gone to all that trouble to lose them at this stage.'

'In God's name! They were — are — yours. Why this ridiculous charade?'

'Because, strange as it evidently appears to you, they are very far from being mine. They belong to my father,' he grated, lashing her feet, separately, to the front legs of the chair. 'That makes a significant difference, unfortunately.'

'And you're after selling them? Family heirlooms. How despicable!'

'Yeah,' he said crudely. 'Brings a tear to my eye, and a lump to my wallet.'

'You'll be found out. Caught.'

'You think so?' His voice was smooth. 'No, my dear, I have no intention of being 'caught', as you put it. Understand that. And walk carefully.' He showed very white teeth. 'As for our heirlooms — well, I'm aiming to redress the balance of fortune a little, that's all. Already my father has sold everything saleable to finance his own grandiose schemes. There's virtually nothing left. Except the tapestries. And they were due to go next, to buy rare butterflies, or some such foolery . . . Theda and I stood to inherit damn all — just that great, crumbling house, which is more a liability than an asset . . . ' He gave a last jerk to the knots and cut the twine, slipping the knife back into his pocket. 'Theda and I needed a little something — '

'Stupid place to put it!'

'Frognalls bridge?' His smile was suddenly rueful. 'As it turned out, yes. A bad mistake. But I had planned for the stuff to be collected from its hiding-place that same night, the night of the robbery. It had all been arranged. The pick up, sale — everything. Only, my contact let me down. Badly. Failed to collect the goods. Then the buyer got cold feet, withdrew, and I had to arrange another sale. Not that easy.'

'No?' Elise's tone was dry. 'Why didn't you take the tapestries back home? Hide them in Langdon House?'

'Under my father's nose? You must be joking! Moreover, have you ever tried toting a parcel of rolled up wall-hangings around in secret? They're hardly the most inconspicuous of items — '

'I can imagine . . . You'd need a lorry to transport them, for a start.' Cade's lorry? Elise stared up at him. 'Must you tie me like this?'

He nodded. 'I'm afraid you're going to suffer a few uncomfortable hours until I can find another safe place for my booty.'

'And then?'

'That's entirely up to you,' he said smoothly.

'You'll let me go?'

'Naturally.'

'Aren't you afraid I'll tell everyone what you've done?'

'No. That would be very foolish.' His voice held quiet menace. 'Your word against mine, my dear, and the tapestries will, by then, be safely away from the scene . . . Besides — ' His blue gaze met hers coldly. 'You and Seth are scarcely in any position to cast stones. Remember, Arthur Sullivan's suspicions can be quickly resurrected.' He heard the sharp intake of her breath again, and smiled thinly. 'Yes. I know the man had something on you and your husband; he'd already indicated as much. Not too difficult to discover what, I should think? A bit of judicious digging here and there, a word in the right ear . . . Oh, it would be unwise to cross me, Elise, believe me. Very unwise. I don't wish to hurt you or Seth in any way — if you take my meaning. But I'll break you if I have to.

278

Make no mistake about it.'

Stooping, he picked up a length of thicker cord and set about tying the chair securely to the heavy bench behind her. There was no way in which she was going anywhere. That finished, he stood again and gave her a long, hard-eyed stare.

'Well,' he said, 'you and Seth have posed me a problem. Not an insurmountable one, luckily, but one of considerable nuisance value — Hell, Elise, why did you have to meddle?'

She returned his outburst with a wan smile as she watched him begin to tear a piece of rag into strips which, she guessed, would be used to gag her.

'It was a sheer accident,' she said, not entirely with truth. 'The finding of those tapestries. Seth saw you move that dead boy — young Robin Goode . . . '

'A-ah.'

'We wondered why you'd done it — shifted his body from the bridge, I mean — what had you to hide?' She flicked a glance up at him. 'It occurred to me that you might have been, somehow, to blame for the child's death; had hit

him with the Land-Rover, or something — '

'What nonsense.'

'That's what Seth said, too. He was up
in a tree, saw you by the river. Said you'd
had nothing to do with the boy's
accident.'

'No. That was just his, and my, bad
luck. I had gone down to the river to
check that the stuff was all right. We'd
had a lot of rain and I wondered if there
was a chance of water seepage from
above. But everything looked okay. I was
just about to clamber up the river bank
again when that child came racing down
the hill. He shot across the bridge and his
bicycle just . . . well, buckled under
him — ' Lance's gaze sought Elise's.
'Sounds weird, I know. But that's what
happened. One minute he was going like
a bat from hell; the next, the whole frame
of the bicycle seemed to crumple and
collapse, and the boy pitched violently
forward, hitting his head a resounding
thwack on the wall. Broke his neck. He
was dead before I got to him.'

Elise made no comment. She was

staring at him mutely, her face as white as chalk.

'I suppose I panicked,' Lance went on. 'Anyhow, I picked him up and put him in my Land-Rover, and carted him off elsewhere. To a ditch along the Hatchins road, as it turned out. You see, I couldn't risk police maybe investigating the Frognalls area; not with my tapestries still in that bridge conduit.' He approached her, the strip of torn cloth dangling from his hand.

Shaking her head from side to side, Elise whispered, pleadingly: 'No.'

'Necessary, I'm afraid.'

With ungentle fingers, he bound her mouth.

Elise stared up at him in helpless protest, eyes wide and gold-green above the grimy rag.

'Time to go,' he said. He smiled at her, a slow and crooked smile. 'Be a good girl, now — ' And he went out and closed and fastened the door. She heard the padlock rattling noisily against its chains.

Long after he had gone, she sat there, numbed, unwilling even to turn her head.

Hot silence, broken only by the frantic struggles of a butterfly trapped against the dirty window. Strand by strand, its fluttering wings tore the cobwebs from across the pane until they hung in ugly, long grey tatters. Slowly, the smell of the building seeped into her consciousness. A rich compound of sun-baked wood and musty string and old rags, of damp soil and green leaf and decay. Something, too, that she didn't like: a suggestive odour of dead things. And, still, silence.

Then, far off, from somewhere near the southern woods, there came the starting rumble of a lorry engine, followed by its swelling progression along the drive, past, and dwindling again to nothingness.

Experimentally, Elise twisted her hands against her bonds. Useless. The knots were firm, as she had guessed. Lance had tied her with scientific care. The twine, though, was old. Again, she fought against it. Old, but used in more than sufficient quantities to hold her secure, and all that parted was the tender skin of her wrists. Better, far, to possess herself in patience, and wait. For Lance. Or Seth.

Her eyes flicked to the window. Would Seth come? Doubtful. At least, he'd not consider searching for ages yet. More to the point, would Lance let him come? Or had Lance lied? Was her husband already being maltreated, bound, as she had been? Frantically, her hands tussled once more against the restraining cords. But only her bracelet worked itself free, to dangle irritatingly across her hand, hampering her efforts even further.

She bit against the gag. That, too, was tight. Hot. Sweat was beginning to trickle in her armpits and down her face. No possibility, though, of wiping it away.

Her gaze returned to the window. Nothing to see. An empty drive, shimmering; vistas of long grass and daisy-headed ragwort, green and gold and unstirring under the motionless, heavy heat. Specks of dust danced before her eyes. The butterfly had set up its futile flapping again. Up and down, with a beat of wings like the shake of dry leaves. Elise watched, hypnotized. There was nothing else to do.

Then, beyond, a sudden — different — movement.

Someone was coming along the driveway.

Elise stared, almost disbelieving. Cliff Burns, a shopping-bag swinging merrily from his handlebars, was cycling up towards Langdon House.

But there was no way of attracting his attention.

Her frantic eyes circled the hut.

Soon he would be past, and gone . . . But he had to come back again, she knew. So, what? What? She stared around again. What was there to use to gain his notice?

Nothing within reach of her grasping fingers, Lance had made sure of that.

Flower-pots, boxes, tins — all too far away to knock to the floor, or kick, or throw. Throw? If she could just get something within her clutches —

Over by the window, on the sill, a familiar object, covered in cobwebs — Seth's old rabbit-catcher, his *bolas*, abandoned there and long forgotten — but, again, too far away for her to reach. Frustration almost made her cry.

Yet the sight of that primitive hunting weapon produced the worm of an idea. If she could slip the bracelet off her wrist . . .

A few more frantic twists and tugs and the heavy jet lumps on their silver chains were dangling from her fingers. Now, she had her own *bolas*. She tried an experimental swing or two. Weighty, enough — if she could just get the trajectory right . . . Difficult, though. With her wrists bound behind her back, her hands and fingers had only limited movement. She began another swing.

Round and round the bracelet whirled, gaining momentum with every circuit until she could feel the savage drag of the stones against her hand.

Her eyes on the road, she twirled the missile and waited . . . Waited . . .

And Cliff Burns was cycling back. Now!

With pent breath, Elise abruptly released her hold on the spinning bracelet and it shot like a bullet towards the window. There was an explosive crack as it struck its target, and the window shattered.

Swerving wildly, Cliff Burns brought his machine to a standstill and stared, open-mouthed, across at the shed.

For one heart-stopping moment, Elise thought he was going to leave it at that, that he was going to remount and pedal off, but, after a second's deliberation, the boy lowered his bicycle to the grass and began to walk slowly in her direction. When he reached the shed, he stood on tiptoe and peered in curiously through the broken window.

Then, with the sparkling response of a true Chatton Eastwoodian, he growled: 'Whatever are you doing in there, Elise?'

18

Once through the gap of the window — a double climb for Cliff Burns, who had had the sense to knock the jagged glass from the frame with the heel of his shoe before clambering in to release her — Elise made for the lower field path, which would bring her out by a stile just above the bridge at Frognalls. It was a slightly longer route home than the usual short cut via Drearden's Wood, but she could hardly abandon Cliff and his bicycle without some sort of explanation. Her trussed-turkey routine in the potting-shed must have appeared distinctly odd. At least, this way, she could walk a distance with him, collect her scattered wits and cobble up a plausible story for him to tell his family, his cronies and anyone else who chose to listen. She could also, she hoped, check on the tapestries at the bridge, see if Lance had removed them. If not . . . She sighed beneath her breath. That would bring its own problems.

Biting her lip, she glanced covertly at the boy by her side. But what to say? The truth was out: she was sure that Lance would keep his promise and retaliate in like manner if she or Seth attempted to squeal on him ... In the end, she laughingly admitted to having played a game; one that had been rough and silly and had got out of hand —

Maybe Cliff believed her.

Anyhow, he gave her a cheery enough wave as he cycled away.

Frognalls bridge was deserted and the roll of tapestries had gone. That much Elise could tell from the river-bank. Nothing to be seen there now but the gaping circular entrance to the vacant conduit. Daylight, a small spherical gleam at the far end.

Above the brickwork, gold threads of sunshine trailed the evening sky.

The shadow of the bridge lay black across the water. There, by the cutwaters, the deeper flow was always cold. Elise shivered. The air was heavy with the lingering smell of sun-dried grass and flowers, and, overhead, swallows skimmed and darted in the last warmth of sunset. In Lance's words, it was time to go.

She turned her tired feet towards the roadway, where ranked thistles in tall, full purple bloom guarded the verge like spearmen, piercing her skin and releasing their almondy scent as she brushed past them.

Behind her, the watchtower frowned down at her for a moment, then, as she rounded the bend, dropped abruptly from sight. The rutted, weed-grown stretch of carttrack traversed, and she was home.

Seth was waiting for her in the kitchen.

'You took your time,' he said. 'Supper's ready. Tea's freshly brewed.' Lifting the teapot, he stood it on its silver tripod on the table.

He had a look of suppressed excitement, a glow in him like a thousand-watt light-bulb, incandescent, heated, too brilliant, almost, for safety.

'Where's Kathie?' Elise dropped wearily into a chair.

Seth nodded towards the closed door

beside the stairs. 'In her bedroom.'

'Good.' Accepting a cup of tea, Elise began rapidly to relate her dealings with Lance and her subsequent escape.

'He's taken the tapestries,' she said.

'He's welcome to them,' replied Seth. His eyes glowed green as emeralds across at her.

'You don't seem too concerned.'

He grinned. 'I'm not. After I left you, I went back to the bridge — '

'Frognalls?' Her head shot up. 'Did you see Lance?'

'No. Should I have?'

'He was heading that way when he departed. How long were you there?'

'A few minutes, no more — ' He glanced across at her. 'Just long enough, anyway, to take another look at those tapestries — '

She stared at him, brows lifted.

'That's right.' His voice held barely contained excitement. 'I pulled them out again, opened them up — '

'In heaven's name, why?'

'Because,' he said with a widening grin. 'Do you remember, this afternoon, in the sandpit, how I was writing our names? *Seth and Elise*, all linked together? Then *SandE*?'

She nodded.

'And do you recall, as well, how I went on to erase that final E? . . . Suddenly, the characters appeared to make quite different sense. *Sand*. A perfectly proper word in its own right. Anyone coming into the sandpit at that point would have imagined that was what I had been writing. Sand.'

'So?'

'*Adamant*. Think about it. It never did make sense. Not coming, as it did, from an ignorant little country girl. Not as another name to describe the diamond, nor yet as a bald statement of her obvious courage . . . So, what else could the Langdon maid have been writing in her own blood?' He eyed her in triumph. 'Adam and Eve, of course. She was trying to tell her master to examine the tapestry. The one they call The Expulsion from Eden. *Adam and Eve* was what she was scrawling, with the letters running together as mine had done in the sandpit . . . Only, her strength gave out before she finished. The final word was missing entirely, while the *d* of the *and* had been crossed like a *t* — most probably as she collapsed across it, smearing the still-wet blood with her hand . . . '

He unclenched his own hand and held it out to her.

'Proof positive,' he said. On his palm, a diamond the size of a small egg winked up at them.

'The Langdon diamond,' breathed Elise. She touched it with a tentative finger. 'In the tapestry?'

'That's right.' He gave her a crooked grin. 'In the belly of the quaintly pregnant Eve. A long shot, that. I'd never known her depicted in that condition elswhere. Although all the figures in the Langdon design are somewhat, well . . . well-rounded. Even the damned angel looks five months gone — '

'Obviously the fashion-fetish of the time. But, even so, I wonder why no one noticed?'

'Hanging, I doubt if it were really very noticeable. Or perhaps the tapestry was

just too darned familiar. After all, no one heeds the old wallpaper on the wall . . . '
He held the diamond to the light, gloating over the coloured fire which coruscated from every facet. 'Beautiful . . . and costly . . . ' He twisted the gem. 'And mine.'

'Yours? Don't be so ridiculous!'

With a jerk of his head he turned to look at her.

'Ours, then. We're rich.'

'It belongs to the Langdons. We have to give it back.'

'Not likely.' His hand snapped shut on the diamond. 'After what Lance did to you? We sure as hell owe *him* nothing . . . He has his tapestries; let him be satisfied. Besides, he doesn't know we have this. No one knows.'

'I know. Now. And I say we give it back.'

'No.'

'Seth. You've had your share of luck, with Amos. Don't push it.'

He stared at her sullenly. 'This is part payment on all the lousy deals Kathie and I've suffered over the years. Compared

293

with us, Lance and Theda have had life bloody cushy.'

'So? You still can't keep the Langdon diamond. Apart from any moral issues involved, you'd never be able to dispose of the stone satisfactorily. Questions would be asked, you'd be found out — ' She contemplated with dismay the immediate, obstinate tightening of his jaw. 'Seth!'

'I'm going to give it a whirl, anyhow. Lance has enough to do, keeping his own nose clean. He's not so lilywhite, not by a long road, as we both well know. What with crooked transactions with tapestries, and illegally shifting that boy's body — '

Elise threw him a wintry smile. 'And that's another thing. Lance told me what really happened at the bridge that day; the day Robin Goode was killed.'

'I told you what happened. I saw it.'

'I know you did. But now I've heard the other side. Lance's side. Lance told me — inadvertently, I admit — how the child really died.'

'I told you — '

' —That the boy skidded and went out

of control and hit his head on the wall by Frognalls?'

'That's right.'

'Is it?' She regarded him with narrowed eyes. 'Only, Lance says that Robin didn't actually skid; that the bike frame buckled beneath him, and he was pitched forward against the stonework — a different matter entirely.'

Seth scowled at her for a long minute in silence. Then said: 'Who're you going to believe, then?'

'In this instance? Oddly enough, Lance.'

The breath hissed between his teeth. 'Charming!'

'Buckled, Seth! In the same way that Jonathan Oake's invalid chair buck-led . . .' She gazed bitterly across at him, the expression in her eyes a daunting mixture of pain and anger and total condemnation. 'You killed that child, Seth. You killed Robin Goode. By a form of remote control, in fact. Oh, no one would ever be able to make it stick, it's too bizarre, but I know, and you know, that you sat up in that tree and somehow willed the accident to happen. Deliberately used that Devil-given gift of yours to crumple the framework of his bicycle. And for why? Because he in some way annoyed you? Because he had been tormenting Kathie? Something of the kind.'

Seth's eyes swivelled and rested on the darkening garden for a moment. His mouth had gone dry, but he struggled to make his voice sound as normal, as unworried, as possible.

'It was an accident,' he said.

'I don't doubt it. I'm sure his death wasn't planned. Even I don't consider that you intentionally aimed to murder the boy — I imagine you wanted to hurt him a little, give him a fright, teach him a lesson . . .'

'It was an accident,' repeated Seth stubbornly. 'I admit that thoughts of a similar nature were buzzing through my brain when he cycled down the hill — he'd been a positive little pest for weeks — but, no. I didn't use my . . . the power on him. The whole thing was an accident.' He clung to the shred of a hope that she would believe him.

'You mean, your metal-bending ability — got away from you?' She looked at him uncertainly. 'Can it do that? Go rogue? . . . Can a mere stray wish trigger it off? Is that what happened that day?'

'Something like that.' He breathed more freely. She'd never forgive him for deliberately engineering the death of a child. 'I imagine,' he said painfully, 'that, deep inside, I had grown so angry with the lad — '

Her eyes flicked him like whips. 'And if ever I make you as angry — ? What then?'

He flinched back from her as if she had struck him.

Elise went on, in that cold, stabbing little voice: 'What would you do? Punish me, too? Scald me with boiling oil from a collapsing pan? Drop a heavy picture on my head? Tighten the chain of my medallion around my throat — ?'

His own throat had constricted almost too much to allow speech, but he forced out the words.

'You,' he said, 'I could never hurt.'

'No?' Sarcastic. 'How can I be sure?

Suppose one day I make you extremely angry? Upset you in some terrible way?'

He stared at her helplessly. 'I love you. I would never harm you. Surely you must realize that? No matter what you did . . . '

'Yet, in sudden rage, you might maim me, or even kill me — by accident.'

'No!' He compressed his mouth. 'You don't understand. It's not like that. The powers I have, they must be firmly directed to an end. It takes time, effort, the force of will. I have to concentrate . . . to control . . . '

His voice died away into the utter silence. Out of his own mouth, he stood condemned. And no way, now, of recalling the words. He bowed his head.

Elise thought that he must surely hear the loud stuttering of her heart as she strove for command over her shaking body, and guessed that always, subconsciously, she must have known the truth. Must have been aware of it long before Lance Langdon had confirmed her unfaced fears. It was too useful a gift not to be used for Seth's own ends. Before her inward eye the afternoon's misadventure concerning Jonathan Oake again flashed plain. That event had scarcely been due to an unconcentrated, passing whim. She had seen Seth's face, stared into his eyes, had recognized the immense effort being put forth by his mind. Looking back, now, she knew that she had been unsurprised. There was, too, earlier still, the incident with the axe that had sliced Sullivan's leg — Arthur'd blamed her. Elise. The witch. But she'd suspected, even then, the truth.

Her lips curved sourly. She wondered if Seth realized just how dangerous he was; a kind of perambulating bomb. Within him, the ability to wreck, to cripple, to destroy, merely by a twist of his mind. No need for recourse to tools, equipment, plans or paraphernalia; he could simply use whatever was — metallically speaking — readily to hand. Or brain! Again her mouth took on that sour curve. And no one's home was safe from him, because he was able to enter and leave as he pleased. Locks, bolts, bars, behaved like putty before him.

Became useless. Cheap bent toys. Fleetingly, she wondered about his range. Limited, she would imagine, but doubted whether it had ever been put to the test.

So much that had never been put to the test.

She gave a faint shudder. He would listen to her because he loved her, but if ever he did not — Again, that faint brush of fear across her nape. No wonder Amos had tried to beat the strange ability out of him, had called him the Devil's spawn . . .

Perhaps something of her thoughts reached across to him, because he suddenly looked up and said, with a spark of anger: 'We are as we're born. It's all handed down to us, in one way or another, whether we want it or not, like brown eyes, or red hair, or big ears. I didn't ask to be able to bend metal with my mind — '

Was that what their common and notorious great-grandmother and her daughter, Elise's grandmother, had done? Elise wondered. Was that the foundation of their reputation for witchcraft? Possibly.

She frowned. 'You don't have to do it.' Her hand fiddled with her teacup.

'You don't *have* to see or hear, I suppose, but it'd be damned difficult not to. Stupid, as well.' A faint smile. Then, wheedlingly: 'It doesn't need to be a bad thing, does it? I'm no more likely to kill again than you are, Elise. A man with a knife can be as dangerous.'

But that, too, he had had. And used.

'You killed that child,' she repeated flatly. 'Maybe you didn't intend him to die, but it was your fault; you brought the tragedy about — through sheer malice. And you didn't stop there. You tried the same thing again with Jonathan Oake. Tell me, how many 'accidents' will there have to be before you learn your lesson?'

He was young, and easily provoked, not yet able to control his emotions fully. The spark of anger in him, flared. Burned. He swung on her in swift retaliation.

'None of it was any nastier, I should have thought,' he snarled, 'than bashing an old man's head in. And that

301

deliberately, and with cunning fore-thought — '

Her hand on the teacup stilled.

' — And then,' he went on, bitingly, 'dragging his senseless body into the water and leaving him there, face down, to drown . . . That was what you did, wasn't it, to Arthur Sullivan? . . . So don't come any of your pious claptrap with me! Set us side by side, you and I, Elise, and there's precious little to choose between us.'

The bitter voice poured over her like acid, scarring . . .

Yet, whatever he had done, whatever he did, she loved him. She would lie for him, cheat for him —

And, yes, if necessary, kill for him.

But was he worth it? . . . And where would it end?

She looked up at him through the splinters of her tears.

'You knew,' she said.

'Of course I knew. One can't live with a woman, eat with her, sleep with her, and not know when she's humming like a harpstring. Besides — ' teeth white in a

302

bitter smile, ' — not very subtle to spike my bedtime cocoa. I went out like a light. But Kathie in the morning, informed me that you had left the house. Later, I guessed why.'

'You never said anything.'

'What would words have achieved? I thought you'd prefer it if I didn't know. So I kept quiet. At least, till you chose to tell me of your own free will.' His eyes glinted dangerously. 'But I'll not have you tub-thumping virtue at me when you're as guilty as I am.'

'I did it for you,' choked Elise. 'Arthur Sullivan came here again, threatening to tell the police what he knew, what he suspected. Said he could drop them a hint, anonymously, and that it would be enough to set them digging. I was afraid he might be right. I gave him money, but I knew he'd be back. He had to be stopped . . . '

'So you stopped him — permanently.' A flicker of a smile. 'For that I should be grateful. But I can do my own dirty work, very ably, as you've kindly pointed out . . . So you will sit there and listen to me and do as I say — ' Eyes, now, ice-cold. 'And keep your sodding trap shut — about Amos, about Sullivan, about the diamond, about the accidents . . . about everything. Because you are as bloody-handed as I am.'

'And if I don't?' She was crying openly now, the tears welling and dropping beyond her control.

He wanted to say, Love, don't cry, it's all right; everything will be all right: but he couldn't. Instead he said: 'Would you like a little demonstration?'

No sooner had he finished speaking than, with spectacular effect, the silver tripod collapsed and sent the teapot tumbling towards her. A stream of hot liquid shot across the table and dribbled to the floor, narrowly missing her bare arm.

She stared for a silent second at the steaming chaos, then lifted her eyes.

'You . . . devil!' she choked.

An end? There never would be any end. Not to this. Not to any of it. Once one had put hand to the plough there was no turning back. She knew that now.

Suppose their security were threatened again? What would they do? Two of a kind, Seth had said. Both with that dreadful, inborn predilection towards deceit and violence to get their way. In any way ... The rising hysterical sobs were tearing terrifyingly at reason ... What kind of monsters were they? And, with such a joint inheritance, what kind of monster had she cradled within her? God, some disasters could be righted, but surely not this one. She groped blindly towards the door.

Seth was still staring, almost stupefied, at his handiwork, his anger dead as suddenly as roused.

As Elise wrenched the door-handle and stepped out, he let her go, merely lifting his head to gaze after her with sick eyes. Only when the outer door had slammed behind her did he stumble to his feet.

Kathie was standing in the inner doorway.

Seth regarded her for several seconds without speaking, then, with a visible effort, gathered together his physical resources and flung himself across the room and through the door after Elise, aware that there was no punishment on earth that would compare with losing her.

He tore as fast as he could down the familiar carttrack, cutting away at an angle across the scrubland to try and head her off, and travelling over the rough ground in the poor light at a speed which was risking a broken ankle in his belated attempt to catch her.

Moving instinctively, the tears cold on her cheeks like rain, Elise had already reached the hard surface of the road and was running along it at an equally breakneck pace towards the bridge, and the watchtower beyond . . .

Kathie came forward into the room, slender arms showing in the wide sleeves of her cotton housegown. She had heard every word, and she could guess where Elise, in so demented a frame of mind, had gone.

And she knew what Seth would do.

He would pick up the pathetic bundle of broken bones from the foot of the tower and bury them safely within its walls.

There must be no probing. No questions. No, *why*?

'She flew like a bird,' he would say . . . If, or when, they asked him.

To the Reverend Oake, or some other paramour, they'd probably believe. Convenient.

Shaking fingers pressed on exhausted eyes.

She failed to hear the small car that drew up beyond the hedge, failed to hear the footsteps that stopped at the still open door.

The police constable tapped, peered in.

Without much difficulty, he identified the girl before him. Poor little devil, he thought, recalling the current stories about her. Some kids sure got a rough ride.

'Excuse me, Miss,' he said. 'Sorry to trouble you, but was that your sister-in-law I passed on the road back there? I'm afraid I couldn't — '

Unnerved, Kathie stared wild-eyed at the blue uniform.

He began again. 'May I have a word? . . . With Mr Seth White, then, perhaps —?'

Kathie gave a soft mewl of fear. Not Seth. No!

'She did it,' she babbled hysterically. 'She hit Arthur. She did it . . .'

The policeman stared back at her. What can of domestic worms had he opened here?

But he recognized distress when he saw it.

He was young, and kind-hearted, and he had a kid sister himself, about the same age as this . . .

'Tell me,' he said. He sat without invitation and, groping in a pocket, decanted its contents on to the table in front of him. Legacy of Mr Burns and son, and their tale of a broken window . . . he'd had to check that out, too. With a stifled sigh he turned once more towards the girl; another precious half hour down the drain, he supposed . . .

And he'd only come to return a bracelet —

We do hope that you have enjoyed reading this large print book.

Did you know that all of our titles are available for purchase?

We publish a wide range of high quality large print books including:

Romances, Mysteries, Classics
General Fiction
Non Fiction and Westerns

Special interest titles available in large print are:

The Little Oxford Dictionary
Music Book, Song Book
Hymn Book, Service Book

Also available from us courtesy of Oxford University Press:

Young Readers' Dictionary
(large print edition)
Young Readers' Thesaurus
(large print edition)

For further information or a free brochure, please contact us at:

Ulverscroft Large Print Books Ltd.,
The Green, Bradgate Road, Anstey,
Leicester, LE7 7FU, England.
Tel: (00 44) **0116 236 4325**
Fax: (00 44) **0116 234 0205**

DR. MORELLE TAKES A BOW

Ernest Dudley

Miss Frayle, no longer employed by psychiatrist and detective Dr. Morelle, now works as secretary to Hugo Coltman, head of a drama school. Endeavouring to entice her back, Dr. Morelle accepts an invitation to lecture at the school, only to become entangled in the sinister schemes that threaten the lives of students and teachers. After a brutal murder, tension mounts as Dr. Morelle and Miss Frayle find themselves targeted by the killer. Can Dr. Morelle's investigation be successfully concluded, and the murderer unmasked?

BURY BY NIGHT

Lorette Foley

As the seaside village of Gifford basks in the June sun, the peace is shattered when the body of Simon Connolly is discovered, buried in another person's grave. Who struck him down, and what has become of his fiancée, Lily Sullivan? Detective Inspector Moss Coen arrives from Dublin, with his assistant, to investigate. When two people die suddenly and violently, Geraldine Lovell — Connolly's former fiancée — becomes involved . . . The solution eventually becomes clear — but not before the Inspector's assistant, Finnbarr Raftery, comes close to a watery end.

FLASHPOINT

John Russell Fearn

Gordon Drew's return to his home town coincides with a baffling series of fires and murders. Drew finds himself secretary to a Dr. Carruthers, an eccentric scientist and investigator, who helps the police solve the mystery of the fires. Meanwhile, Superintendent Denning's methodical investigations lead him to the arsonist. However, when he also discovers a ruthless murderer who exploits science to dazzling effect in his crimes, it is Dr. Carruthers who excels and helps Denning bring justice to the criminal.

A TIME FOR MURDER

John Glasby

Carlos Galecci, a top man in organized crime, has been murdered — and the manner of his death is extraordinary . . . He'd last been seen the previous night, entering his private vault, to which only he knew the combination. When he fails to emerge by the next morning, his staff have the metal door cut open — to discover Galecci dead with a knife in his back. Private detective Johnny Merak is hired to find the murderer and discover how the impossible crime was committed — but is soon under threat of death himself . . .